Gold Coin

RENA PILLAI

ISBN: 9789811830822 (Digital)

ISBN: 9789811832840 (Paperback)

Any references to historical events, real people or real places are used fictitiously. Names, characters, and places are the products of the author's imagination.

Book Design by Lisa Rena Raveendran.

First Digital Edition 2021.

This book was self-published by Lisa Rena Raveendran, writing under a pen name, Rena Pillai. For publishing enquiries, please reach out to pillairena@gmail.com.

Gold Coin

Contents

Disclaimer

This is a work of fiction. It does not seek to offend anyone or any belief systems that one might ascribe to. The places and events may reflect the socio-political situation in the year 2014, when the violence was rife between the Muslim and Buddhist extremist groups, but the content itself is not based on real events. The main languages in this book (although written in English) are Burmese and Thai. Please keep an open mind, after all, it's a work of fiction. Enjoy.

For Lydia & Ravi

Gold Coin

Prologue.

All her life she had a simple dream. She just wanted to love and to be loved.

The road to love was not easy, it never was. Life itself was never easy. But she held onto the things she loved, the people she loved and the memories she had, of a time when she was happy. She looked over at a clock in her study and felt that the time she had on this earth was coming to an end. She got up from the swivel chair and placed her reading glasses on the desk. She picked up a small, black journal from the desk and clutched it tightly.

'Oh, darling. What I would give to see you again,' she whispered, as she thumbed through its pages to find a small, faded photograph of a memory of the person she once loved. She then toyed around with a small gold coin around her neck and she smiled to herself.

'You are always here with me, aren't you?' she mused, looking at the photograph.

At that moment, she felt as light as the air around her, falling into a graceful slumber. The world around her began to fade away. And although she heard a thud as her vision began to blur, she could still see a young man urgently running to her.

'Mama! Mama!' she heard him shout, but she felt he was so far away from her.

'Somebody call 999!' she heard another voice.

'This one sounds very anxious,' she registers.

Closing her eyes, she succumbed to the dark world

around her.

'I'm coming to see you, my love,' she heaved a final

whisper.

The darkest night.

It was a cold, rainy night. There was heavy traffic and the streets of Pyay road were beginning to flood. There were rickshaw pullers flocking for shelter. There were masses of cars, headlights, illuminating the heavy rain droplets. Pedestrians were running across the street, running home, away from the rain, and the cars, trying to avoid accidents through the roads that lacked proper traffic control.

A mother had found herself in the same position, as a pedestrian in precarious road traffic conditions. She was cradling her baby - a baby boy, with chubby cheeks and a slightly serene gaze on his little face. He also had a small, yet conspicuous birthmark below his left eye. He was fast asleep, nestled in a *sarong* bundle wrapped around his mother's upper torso.

She ran across the street, to the side of a run-down

shopping lane. She approached an alleyway. It was

quiet, except for the sound of the pitter-patter of the

rain. She then stopped walking as she approached the

corner, near the back entrance of a Buddhist monastery

which was perched on higher ground, avoiding the

flood. She tearfully looked at her baby for one last time

and kissed him on his forehead. He twitched a little, as

she wrapped the *sarong* around him. She bundled him

up until he was entirely shielded from the rain. She

then gently placed him atop the steps, under a shelter,

regretfully turning away. She dried her eyes with a small

floral handkerchief, as she disappeared back into the

rain.

The morning after.

It was a slightly humid morning, with pale clouds hanging low, over the city.

There was a Buddhist monk by the name of U Chin. He was slightly plump, bald and had a kindly face that people felt a sense of peace from just looking at him. He had an empty wooden bowl, carved with intricacies, cradled in his arms. His fingers held a silver tin container of porridge and pickled vegetables. It was a food offering from a pastor's home. He held the silver tin and bowl tightly.

His mind was not at rest. There were rumours going round about religious violence. He was no doubt good friends with the pastor, who never failed to give him a meal every day. He was worried that this harmonious relationship would become strained. He walked towards the monastery's back entrance, barefooted and with calloused feet, taking the shorter route so that he could reach faster for he was already very hungry from the long walk. He was, no doubt thankful for the food, so graciously prepared by his friend, but it was this inconvenience of distance from the monastery to the house that troubled him.

As he approached the steps, he saw a bundled *sarong*. Puzzled by what he saw and curious to take a closer look, he placed the bowl and the tin on the step as he picked up the bundle and unwrapped the *sarong*. To his surprise, he saw a baby.

His eyes widened to take a closer look. He could not believe his eyes. Was he becoming delirious? Yes - he was hungry, but was the hunger going to his brain and causing him to imagine things? He took a final look around, and the weight of the baby was getting to his strength. The baby let out a shrill cry.

'Yup, this is for real,' he thought to himself. 'This is a real baby alright,' chuckling at the thought of his own hallucination.

He nestled the baby in one hand, picking up his bowl and tin in another. He pushed open the back door of the monastery and walked in.

"Teacher," one of the younger monks said, greeting him with a right-angled bow, and palms placed together in reverence.

"Ashoka," he responded.

Ashoka looked up at U Chin. His eyes darted back and forth as he looked at the baby cradled in U Chin's arms. Ashoka evidently looked confused.

"Teacher, is that a baby?" Ashoka asked.

"Yes, my boy, I saw him outside, on the steps of the entrance, round the back," U Chin replied.

Ashoka nodded his head, still confused. "Truly, you are what they say, you are the store of compassion," Ashoka said.
U Chin nodded his head and handed his wooden bowl and tin to Ashoka. "We need to feed the baby," he said to Ashoka.

"Yes, Teacher. But how?" came the concerned reply. "We've never had a baby here before!"

U Chin walked into the dining area and motioned
Ashoka to place his tin of food and bowl on the table.

"I know that babies need milk," he muttered to
himself. 'But we don't have any here!' he thought.

He was still cradling the baby in his arms and walked
slowly to the back entrance and out of the monastery.
There were shops there that he could go to, to buy
some milk for the baby. He walked down the slope and
to the shops. By this time, the baby was asleep. He
walked down to the grocery store and asked the
shopkeeper for some milk.

"For you, Teacher, no cost," the shopkeeper insisted,
even though U Chin offered to pay.

He took the milk from the shopkeeper.

"Hang on a minute," the shopkeeper told U Chin as he walked to the back of his shop. A while later, the shopkeeper came out with a plastic bag.

"What's this?" U Chin asked, his mind still reeling from the excitement of finding the baby.

"Why Teacher! They are necessities for the baby! Pampers and a feeding bottle for the little one you have in your arms! My wife insisted that you come here when you need more supplies for your *little one!*" the shopkeeper replied with a hearty laugh.

"Thank you, sir. May you be blessed for all the kindness you have shown to this humble servant," U Chin said as he gave a slight bow of appreciation.

He proceeded out of the store, heading up the slope to the monastery; with all the supplies he needed to care for the 'little one', as the shopkeeper put it.

As his 'little one' - whom he had named Wunna, got older, U Chin found himself constantly running after Wunna. There were times that U Chin wondered if he was just getting old. It was exhausting, running after Wunna. Wunna was always following him or playing with the other younger kids in the monastery. The teacher loved the boy dearly, having sworn to himself from the very first night he spent in full wakefulness as he watched Wunna gulp down milk in his feeding bottle, that he would take care of Wunna at all cost, even to the point of death.

It was a struggle for U Chin to take care of Wunna only because he was no match for what Wunna's biological mother could have done. Besides, he had no clue on how to take care of a baby. The first few months were indeed challenging with the sleepless nights he endured as Wunna sought attention many times in the night. Thereafter, it was helping him walk and then, to talk. But, be that as it may, U Chin nevertheless found it fulfilling watching Wunna's milestones in life and he was glad that he had an opportunity to invest into Wunna's life. He always viewed a new life as a clean slate, a way to start over. So all he hoped for was to be a positive influence on Wunna's life. He wanted to teach him the ways of compassion, kindness and love – love in a way that is pure, that is untainted by lust. Love that knows no boundaries.

As Wunna was growing up, U Chin would bring him to the pastor's house to collect a meal of porridge and pickled vegetables. After he had told the pastor what he had done for Wunna, and the day he found him atop the steps of the monastery, the pastor had encouraged

U Chin by saying that this was the best thing he had ever done, and that others should learn to follow U Chin's example. The pastor had a daughter; about four years of age, whose name was Thanda. She was a very happy-go-lucky, slightly chubby girl, with hazel eyes and fair skin. She was so full of love and in that expression of her affection, she loved to give hugs. When Wunna was five, U Chin had brought Wunna there, to collect their meals. From the first time Thanda set her eyes on Wunna, they had been close companions ever since.

She told her father, "He is my best friend," and proceeded to give Wunna a hug.

Wunna was startled, but when she ran to the courtyard of the house, he would follow after her. The teacher and the pastor watched over them and chuckled at their innocence and play.

"I am glad that they have found a friend in each other,"
U Chin commented.

"Just as we are," said the pastor, putting a friendly arm
around U Chin's shoulder.

The teacher nodded in agreement.

***

Wunna's and Thanda's childish bickering grew into
youthful bliss. Wunna was already seventeen, and
Thanda, sixteen. Wunna had grown into a man, with
sharp features, and large, kind eyes. He was tall, lean
and muscular, as he was very athletic, and was always
on his feet. Thanda had grown, no doubt, slimmer and
slightly tanner, as she was always helping her brother
out in the fields. Thanda had learnt English from her

father; she loved to read foreign books and understood them with her heart and soul. Sometimes she would share stories to Wunna when he came over to collect the meals she dutifully prepared for him and U Chin.

Not long after, the pastor and his wife passed away in a terrible accident which left U Chin in distress for Thanda and her older brother, Ming. U Chin also had to deal with his own feelings of loneliness as he had lost his closest confidant. He told Ming to harvest rice, since the pastor had a small plot of land behind their house. Ming did what he was told as he knew that his father had regarded U Chin as a man of wisdom. U Chin and Wunna would also chip in and help them out every day in the fields when they came to collect their meals. Wunna pitied Thanda, but she seemed very happy whenever he was around.

Thanda always found her comfort in Wunna's presence. There was something about him that made her feel a sense of peace. She had reserved a special place in her heart for him. But it saddened her greatly at the realization that his life is going to be devoted to becoming a monk and the monastery.

One day.

One hot summer's day, Wunna had come over to collect his meal. He found Thanda in the fields, bending over, threshing the wheat. She was adorned in a green button up blouse and a matching green *sarong*. She had a woven farmer's hat over her tied hair. She wiped the sweat off her brow with the back of her hand.

"Thanda!" Wunna called out.

She got up and looked over, only to find Wunna, with a slightly sullen look, waving back at her. He adjusted his tunic and ran his right hand over his shaven head. Thanda dipped her head in acknowledgement of his presence. She went inside the house as Wunna moved to the front porch of the house.

A few minutes later, she came outside to pass the silver

tin container, of his usual meal of plain porridge and

pickled vegetables, to Wunna. She craned her neck to

see behind his shoulder, before she turned to him.

"Wunna, where is U Chin?" she asked.

"He is unwell, he is back at the monastery. A doctor

came by yesterday and said that teacher is not doing

well," he replied feebly.

Tears welled up in his eyes. Thanda placed her hand on

his shoulder, as if, to offer comfort. He looked up at

her, gazing straight into her eyes. Sensing his

discomfort at her touch, Thanda quickly jerked her

hand back.

"Wait here," she lifted a finger and disappeared back

into the house.

Wunna had a few moments of confusion. He could not deny that he liked the feeling of Thanda's hand on his shoulder. It was a pleasure that he had to forgo from his mind.

'I cannot have feelings for Thanda!' he shuddered at the preposterousness of his thoughts.

"Wunna," came a soft voice, interrupting his thoughts.

He turned around to face Thanda. "Yes?" Thanda handed him a small tin container.

"There is some soup here for teacher," she said. "Please give it to him."

He nodded, "thank you Thanda."

She dipped her head and walked back to the fields to thresh the wheat.

Wunna walked away with a heavy heart. He was sad that U Chin, the man who practically raised him; the man who imparted to him wisdom and compassion, was about to leave this life. Wunna was, however, happy that Thanda had graciously prepared U Chin's meal, even if this was going to be his last one. As he walked, he started to think about life and death. He knew that U Chin was going to be reincarnated into someone great, for all the good things he had done, not just for Wunna, but also for Thanda and Ming, and for the other people that he had come into contact with; the peace he had practiced among people of other religions; and how he looked beyond their faith, and saw them for who they were. He helped all of them, selflessly.

Wunna's thought processes at this depressing time were of how life and death would dance together, like lovers in the wind. When life gets tired, death decides that life is no longer of use. Life allows death to overtake. Death. Eternal separation. Yet, the teacher will be reincarnated, till the time comes for his new life to expire.

'I wonder if I will ever meet the reincarnated version of teacher. Maybe I won't. Maybe I never will,' Wunna mused.

Wunna walked towards the monastery. He set everything down on the table at the dining area. He held the soup tin in one hand and rinsed a spoon. He was tired from the long walk from Thanda's house to the monastery, but he chose to feed U Chin before having his meal. He walked into the room where his beloved teacher slept. At his bedside was Ashoka, squeezing water off a cloth rag and placing the rag over

U Chin's forehead.

Wunna bowed his head, acknowledging Ashoka's

presence and walked towards U Chin's bedside.

"Teacher," he said as he kneeled by his bedside.

He stirred the soup as Ashoka helped place more

pillows to allow U Chin to sit up comfortably. Wunna

fed U Chin the soup that Thanda had graciously

prepared, slowly, blowing to prevent the hot soup from

scalding his tongue. There they sat, the three of them,

with Ashoka gently fanning U Chin. After feeding him,

Wunna dipped his head to thank Ashoka.

As Ashoka led him out of the room he remarked to

Wunna, "Wunna, our teacher is dying. The doctor

came back again just about an hour before you came to

feed him. The doctor has given him only a few more hours to live," he said.

Wunna looked at him in shock and disbelief. Tears started to stream down his face as Ashoka broke the bad news. He went back into U Chin's room and held his hand for one last time, thanked him, and made a promise to honour his teachings.

About an hour later, U Chin slipped into a dreamless sleep as his soul left his body.

Days. Hours. Minutes. Seconds.

It had been close to six months after his teacher's death and Wunna was still trying to come to terms with the tragedy. He still continued to head to Thanda's house to collect his daily meal of plain porridge and pickled vegetables. Although life seemed dull for Wunna without U Chin as he performed his daily rituals and duties as a monk, he found a sense of joy in having to go to Thanda's house every day.

'Thanda has been through a tragedy greater than I have,' Wunna mused. 'She lost both her father and mother. I lost my loved one too, my teacher - my father.'

The daily activities had taken much of his time and kept him from focusing on his grief.

One evening, some of the younger monks had gathered in the dining hall. There was a buzz about a war, a riot. They were talking with such valour. Wunna walked into the hall to hear what the commotion was about.

"There has been unrest! We are at war!" said one of the monks. "We need to take a stand, we need to fight!"

There were more chants and swears of a dirty war between the Buddhists and Muslims.

"How could they do this? How could they rape our women? This is an abomination! We need to eradicate them! We will have to fight them!" said one of the monks.

He was young, passionate, hot-headed, and one could even say that he was militant.

"Thiha, my brother, why are you doing this?"

questioned Wunna. "Were we not taught to be peaceful

and loving? Can we fight this without our fists and

bombs?"

"You simpleton. It is not as easy as you think! I heard

from other people, when I was on my way out of the

monastery, that the Muslims are going to kill all of us!

They are after us. Don't you see that, Wunna? We have

to fight them before they come for us!" chimed

another monk.

There were slurs and jeers held at Wunna's stance of

peace.

"There will be war! Let there be unrest! We will prove

to them who we are!" the rest of the monks started to

chant.

Wunna looked at Thiha, "Well, I am not going to be involved in this day of reckoning among us Buddhists and our Muslim brothers."

Wunna looked at him, and the rest of the younger monks angrily, who were evidently on Thiha's side. It was a side that bred violence and hatred; violence that he did not want to be part of. He was glad that his teacher was not alive to see this.

"Brothers? How could you call them brothers?" Thiha shrieked.

"How dare you say that!" Wunna screamed, raising his fist, resisting the urge to punch Thiha.

The room fell into a tense silence. The rest of the monks stopped their chatter while Thiha stood on, scornfully.

"Don't you see that what you're hearing are just rumours and that you are acting on those false stories because you have already made up your mind that our Muslim brothers and sisters are evil? They aren't!" Wunna continued. "And you know what Thiha, you should be ashamed of yourself."

"Drop the good-guy act Wunna," Thiha retaliated. "You will never understand how to fight for what is right."

"Well, I know that violence isn't right," Wunna answered.

"And what if it comes down to your life?" Thiha challenged. "Won't you have to fight for yourself then?"

"It doesn't matter Thiha, even if I die," Wunna shrugged. "Well good luck to you, Thiha, and the rest of you. I would advise you against it. It is all not what we have grown to know. But you have your opinions, and I have mine. I'm not going to be a part of this."

Wunna turned away and walked out of the dining hall. He could hear the younger monks mocking his peace regime, as Thiha continued to incite hatred. But Wunna chose to ignore it.

That night, Wunna lay down on his mat, thinking about the events that reeled earlier in the evening.

'I know that what I'm doing is right,' he thought. 'Thiha is wrong.'

No doubt, Wunna was afraid of the killings that were supposedly going to occur.

'I'm too young to die!' he thought.

He closed his eyes and his mind drifted to thoughts of Thanda. Her smile, her simple life as a farmer, her beauty and grace, all in a small frame and a big heart. 'Thanda, dear sweet Thanda,' he thought.

He drifted off to a deep sleep.

After what seemed like a couple of minutes, Wunna was rudely awakened to the sound of broken glass. He woke up to the dizzying sound of wailing and bullets. He sat up, beads of sweat trickling down his back. He got to his feet and took a look around his room; his fellow roommates were running out of the room. He ran out towards the commotion. There, he saw that some of the older monks were getting beaten up. He saw some of the younger ones running to protect them.

The younger monks had guns in their hands and they did not hesitate to shoot their enemies.

One of the attackers came charging towards Wunna, with a gun in his hand. His face was covered with a cloth, except for his piercing stare. Wunna reacted. He twisted his attacker's arm causing the attacker to inadvertently pull the trigger upon himself.

Time stood still for a moment as a loud blast of the gun filled the room.

Wunna's act of defence killed his attacker.

'I've killed him!' he thought. 'Thiha was right, I am nothing but a murderer.'

 He knelt beside his attacker, his eyes, vacant. 'He's dead, by my hands! What have I done?'

He looked around, still on his knees and saw that a card

had fallen out of this attacker's pocket. He took it and

crawled out of the war zone, back to the kitchen and

finally out of the back door of the monastery.

He stood up and took a deep breath, leaning against

the back door.

'Inhale. Exhale.'

Wunna felt his heart beating out of his chest and he

could hear the rhythmic thumping of his heart in his

ears, as the sounds faded behind him. Composing

himself, he could still hear the shrill cries of the monks

and their attackers, masked and valiant, at war. He tried

to control his breathing as he ran for safety towards a

nearby bridge. Catching his breath, he stood under the

faint lights of the bridge, scrutinizing the card he had

picked up from the attacker. The card itself was stained with blood. He grabbed the excess cloth that hung over his shoulder from the tunic that he had normally worn and tried to wipe the blood off the card. To his surprise, it had the face and the address of the man who tried to kill him.

Run.

Dark clouds hung heavy across the sky. Wunna was running. Running away from what happened, from death, from the perverseness of religion, from hate, and from all the noise. In contrast to the thoughts that plagued his mind, it was a fairly quiet night outside. The village was pin quiet except for the occasional chirps and croaks of cicadas and bullfrogs.

He steadied his pace and breath as he ran, adjusting his tunic every so often. He ran towards the address of his attacker. It was a place that was familiar to him.

'What am I doing?' he asked himself. 'If I seek forgiveness from the family of my attacker, they may kill me! But no! Better for me to die a martyr who seeks forgiveness than an unforgiving killer in the name of religion. Oh what have I done!'

He continued to run.

He reached the clearing of the house. It was dark and there were trees just behind the rusty gate. He opened the gate and walked through the trees. He reached the entrance of the house and knocked on the door, bracing himself for the death that could befall.

There was no reply. He knocked on the door once more. The door opened, with a slight creak. He gently pushed open the door, slightly wider, letting himself in. A dim light, from a naked light bulb, illuminated the room. An elderly woman in a *hijab* was seated on the rocking chair at the side of the small living room. She turned to her side, facing the door that Wunna tried to creep in through.

"Come in, boy," she instructed. He dipped his head and went to her side. She held the smell of fresh sandalwood, seeping through her blouse and *sarong*.

She looked at him, forlorn. "What brings you here, boy? In the dead of night?" she asked him.

He could see that her face was wrinkled and worn out from, probably, months of working in corn or rice fields. She had a kind face, a one that would always be lit with a smile.

Wunna felt a lump well up in his throat. He looked at her, straight into her eyes, and knelt by her side. He looked down at the floor, finding a focal point on a wooden floorboard.

"I...I... killed your son," he finally managed.

He expected her to hit him so hard. Instead, she placed her soft, wrinkled hand on his shaven head. She stroked his head, causing him to look up.

"You…you are not going to kill me?" he asked, perplexed, by her gesture.

She let out a small laugh, "Now, child, why would you think I would do that?"

"I just killed your son" came the baffled reply.

"Yes, yes, I understand," said the old lady. "My son is dead to me. Five years ago, when he chose to walk out of those doors," she motioned to the main door of the house. "He is dead to me. Yes, I hoped that he would come back, change his ways and follow the proper teachings of *Allah*. But no, he wanted to fight. He wanted to cause disharmony, just like how the younger generation decides to misinterpret the words of *Allah,*

all so that they can use it as an excuse to fight, to start

war and unrest. But if *Allah* taught us to love, why

then, do we hate?"

"I..." Wunna's voice trailed off.

"Kid, don't speak. I don't hate you. I know now, my

son did not die because of you. He died because of the

choices he made."

She looked into his kind eyes, begging for forgiveness.

At that moment, she felt something click as she looked

intently at his face with a particular focus on a

conspicuous birthmark below his left eye. She felt a

strong bond with the boy. As she looked on into his

eyes, she remembered that he was the child she once

left on the steps of the monastery many years ago. All

these years she had watched him, from a distance. He had grown into a wonderful man, with a gentle soul.

'*He was raised well,*' she mused. '*More than I could have ever done for him.*'

She blinked and let the tears roll down her cheeks.

"I forgive you, my son," she finally said.

Wunna stared at her in bewilderment. He felt the lump in his throat grow bigger. He swallowed; eventually letting the tears and sadness in his heart go. He wept, burying his face in his hands, as the old lady placed a comforting hand on his shoulder. She then pulled him closer to her.

"Everything is going to be okay," she assured.

She withdrew her hand from him and unhooked the necklace she was wearing. It was a simple gold coin with a small hole in the middle that was fastened on with a black string. She took the coin out of the string.

"Look here, my son," she said, as she gently removed his hands from his face, causing him to look up. She placed the coin on his palms saying, "this coin was given to me by my grandfather before he died. I give this to you because I have no one else to give this to, for I, too, am a dying old woman. This coin has been with me throughout my life. It's to bring you good fortune in everything you do."

She then cupped his face with her hands.

"Take this and remember me," she said.

After that exchange, Wunna ran. Into the darkness of

the night he ran far away.

Thanda.

It was a fairly warm evening. Thanda's heart was heavy after hearing rumours going round the marketplace of a riot that had broken out the day before in the monastery that Wunna resided in. She told Ming about it.

"I know that Wunna is not the type to fight!" she had told Ming earlier that evening.

"But what if he feared for his life and joined the militant monks?" Ming questioned. "There's so much violence between the Muslim and the Buddhist communities going around Thanda, I wouldn't be surprised if he had to join them to save himself."

'What if he's dead?' she thought. Her mind was confused. Her spirit was uneasy, for she feared for Wunna's safety.

"I know the kind of man Wunna is," she told her brother, eventually.

Ming just shrugged, "I'm just saying, Thanda. You may never know."

She lay on her mat, thinking about Wunna, hoping that he was alright. Just as she was about to drift off to a deep sleep, there was a loud bang on the door. Her eyes snapped open. Fearing for her safety, she ran into the adjacent room where Ming was sleeping soundly.

"Ming! Ming!" she whispered, running into Ming's room. "Someone's at the door!" She nudged him to wake up.

"I'm coming, 5 minutes," he groaned and turned.

Another loud bang.

"Ming! I'm serious! Wake up!" She pushed him off his mattress.

He opened his eyes and jolted awake. She grabbed an old cricket bat that was at the corner of the room.

"Here," Thanda anxiously thrusted the bat to her brother.

Ming took the bat, Thanda followed suit. There was another loud bang. The siblings jumped up, startled. Taking deep breaths, they crept to the door and Ming opened it, raising his bat to hit the intruder.

"Please! I come here in peace," the voice cried.

Thanda recognized it immediately.

"Wunna?" A wave of relief swept across her mind, knowing that he was alive.

Wunna crouched, placing his arms over his head, protecting his face. Thanda and Ming looked at each other confused.

"What are you doing here in the middle of the night, Wunna?" Ming asked, lowering the bat and wiping the beads of sweat off his brow.

"I'm sorry, but can I come in?" Wunna asked, regaining his composure.

"Please," Thanda replied, pulling him by the hand into the house.

Ming fumbled with the light switch. Thanda motioned to Wunna to sit. She went into the kitchen to get a glass of water. She set the glass on the rickety, old, wooden coffee table. Wunna gulped it down, for his throat was parched. Ming sat next to him and Thanda found her space next to Wunna.

"I have been on the run," Wunna explained. He narrated the whole story to them, from the time the monastery was attacked to the time he found the old woman who forgave him and kindly sent him on his way. He was scared of the consequences of what he had done. He feared for his life but he also felt guilty for taking the life of his attacker, even though it was done in self-defence.

"I am leaving to find a safe place. I am going to run away from here, far away," Wunna said, eventually.

Thanda could not imagine all that he was saying. She saw the coin and felt the fear in his voice. It was hard to believe he had killed someone, even though it was an accident. Her mind was dizzy with all the information, so she sat there silently, contemplating Wunna's situation.

Wunna stood up to leave, prompting Ming to run into his room to get his wallet.

"Here," Ming said, handing Wunna some money. "You are going to need this to escape."

"Thank you Ming, I will never forget your kindness," Wunna replied.

He looked over at Thanda.

"Thanda, I have to leave. It is for my safety. But I still can't imagine a life spent without you. I am sorry, Thanda." Wunna mustered all the courage he could. "I need you, Thanda. I…I love you."

He turned away and made his way to the front door.

Ming looked at Thanda, quite surprised by Wunna's confession. Thanda stood there, her expression shell-shocked, as Wunna walked out of her house and onto the sandy road.

'Quick! Make a move! *You do want to spend your life with Wunna! Don't you?*' her heart screamed.

As Wunna was making his way out of Thanda's house, trudging slowly through the sandy road, he heard a soft voice at a distance, calling his name.

"Wunna! Wait!" Thanda yelled.

Wunna turned around to see Thanda running, her *sarong* flapping in the wind, arms swinging, with a brown suitcase in one hand. She ran and caught up with him. Adjusting her blouse and her hair, she drew deep breaths.

"Take me with you," she wheezed.

The Journey.

The two of them made their way down the sandy road

walking slowly, in the darkness of the night, There was

neither a watch nor a compass to direct their paths, or

tell them the time.

"How do we know where we are going?" Thanda

asked.

"I follow that big star," Wunna said, pointing up at the

sky.

They continued to walk in silence. It was a warm night,

but the sky was clear, full of stars and the moon sat

high up in the sky. After what seemed like a couple of

hours trekking through the night, Thanda had started

to grow weary. She started having doubts about this

decision of running away with Wunna; she wondered if

she was doing something so crazy and reckless. Yet, it made sense for her to be with him at this moment. The two of them were now walking through the rice fields. Fearing the odd snakes that lay in wait in the dark, Thanda turned to Wunna and said, "Wunna, can we take a break?"

"We can seek refuge there," Thanda pointed to a small concrete shack with a zinc roof by the side of the field. "We can leave before dawn breaks."

Wunna nodded.

"What do you have in that bag?" he asked.

"Why, some money, my favourite book, two toothbrushes, and some clothes of course! There is something in here from Ming. Since we are running away, and you are in hiding, you need to blend in with the crowd," she replied.

"But my shaven head will give it away!" he exclaimed.

"Oh, don't worry." she said, amused by his naivety. "Hair grows. Just stop shaving it for a while."

"Ah well," he shrugged. "Pleasures like this would be forbidden in the monastery."

"Well, you are out of it," Thanda pointed.

A few moments of silence rested between them.

"Will you ever consider going back?" she asked. "To the monastery, I mean, or to any other monastery, for that matter," she added.

"I…I don't know. I can't just leave you, Thanda. Not like this, after all I've been through and after all that has happened. Killing a man – there is no justification for that. I am not worthy of being a monk – or human even," he answered, with tears in his eyes, as his mind reeled back to the events that had transpired.

Thanda squeezed his hand, offering him some comfort.

'It all happened so fast. Just way too fast,' he thought.

They made their way to the shed at the east side of the rice field. There, they rested till dawn.

***

Thanda had woken up early. Looking through the makeshift concrete-cut window frame of the shed, she could see the sky still enveloped in darkness. There were no stars to be seen, the light of the moon had

dimmed a little.

'The sun would be rising soon,' she thought.

She turned and looked at Wunna. He was fast asleep,

still in his maroon tunic, with the coin he talked about,

clasped tightly in his fist.

"Wunna," she gently jostled him awake. "You should

get dressed, we have to leave."

He opened his eyes, orientating himself to the

surroundings. Thanda opened the suitcase and tossed a

tee shirt, a pair of jeans and a pair of sandals next to

Wunna.

"Get dressed, we have to leave," Thanda repeated.

He squinted his eyes and nodded. She walked out of the shed to give him some privacy. When he came out, he looked like a very different man - almost unrecognizable. He was like the Wunna in her growing up years. The clothes fitted him well.

"It feels…weird," said Wunna. "It is uncomfortable, but at least I don't have to keep clutching the coin. These things are useful!" he exclaimed, putting his fist in his pocket to emphasise his point, as he gave Thanda the tunic. He then crammed the coin down the pocket of his jeans.

'This would serve as a reminder of Wunna'a past life,' she mused as she neatly folded and placed the tunic inside the suitcase.

"You will get used to it, eventually," she said.

"Yeah," Wunna replied.

The two of them walked back into the rice fields as they made their way to the other end of the field from the shed, veering through the darkness. Thanda prayed that they would not encounter any snakes or vicious insects on their way out of the field. A while later, they managed to reach an empty plain that rested on slightly higher ground. There, they stopped and watched the sunrise. The sky began to fill with yellowish, orangey hues, making the dark sky look almost pink. The sun began to rise. A new day was dawning.

"It's beautiful, isn't it?" Thanda asked.

"Simply breathtaking," Wunna replied. "This is the best gift given to me, with you by my side. I want to remember this moment forever."

Thanda blushed as they sat side by side. There was still a comfortable distance between them.

Afternoon rolled by. It was a humid afternoon, yet pale clouds hung low over the sky. To their relief, there was an occasional breeze that provided some respite as they continued their journey to another village, not far from the place they stayed the night before. There was a rush of people walking through the sandy streets, passing through the market, where they sold fresh fish, veal, gizzards, fruits, flowers and food. The sights and smells excited Wunna's taste buds, as he was hungry. They hadn't eaten anything since that morning when Thanda found a banana tree and plucked several bananas for them to feast on for breakfast.

"Everything suddenly smells amazing," said Wunna. "What would you like to eat, Thanda?" he asked, turning to look at her, but she was nowhere to be seen.

'Thanda! Thanda! Where are you?' he panicked. 'Just a moment ago, she was here!' his mind reeling with anxiety.

"Hey! Over here!" he heard Thanda shout. "Come here!" he saw her waving vigorously from a florist, beckoning him to come over. His panic subsided as went over to her.

"I thought I lost you!" Wunna exclaimed.

"I'm sorry, I should not have run off like that," she apologized.

"I just got distracted by these pretty flowers," she said, pointing to the orchids.

"It's okay," he replied. Turning to the shopkeeper he asked, "could I have two stalks of these?"

Thanda looked at him, pleasantly surprised at his gesture as she thought he would have reprimanded her for leaving him all alone. He paid the florist quietly and received the flowers that were wrapped tightly in a newspaper bouquet. He handed her the flowers and traded it for the suitcase she was carrying. Thanda looked at him, wonderfully surprised, as a shy smile swept across his face. He looked at the ground, recovering from his reverie.

"Shall we go for lunch?" he asked.

They went to a small street side stall. They both ordered vegetable soup with lentils and rice, and had their meal in silence. As she sat across Wunna, Thanda observed him eating for the first time with her, as he wolfed down his food hungrily. She ate her meal slowly as she watched him.

'He is actually very good-looking,' she observed.

His eyes were a beautiful shade of grey; his shaven head was starting to stubble. His countenance was one of sharp features and his skin was tan, there was a noticeable growth of a beard. Beyond his looks, he was a man of character. A man who stood firm for what he believed.

'It does not matter what he has done. I know he did not intend to kill that man,' she reassured herself.

After lunch, they headed up north, trudging through villages and towns.

"We should get on a train and head to Myawaddy," said Thanda. "From there we can escape to Thailand," she continued. "Once we head to Thailand, we can just start a new life. Nobody will even know who we are!"

The two of them walked towards the train station. Thanda read the chalkboard that presented the prices of tickets to the respective towns.

"Myawaddy…Myawaddy…" Her eyes scanned the board for the price of their proposed destination.

"Hmmm…Myawaddy.. ther- *what*!?!? This is daylight robbery!" she exclaimed, turning to look at Wunna. "It's too expensive for us to get there! We clearly don't have enough money to even head to the last stop of Myanmar."

Thanda went to the counter next to the board and waited in line to speak with the station inspector. After what seemed like an eternity she managed to get her turn to speak with him. The station inspector seemed annoyed when she came to him with her request.

"Excuse me, can I just ask you if you have a cheaper train ticket to Myawaddy?" she asked sweetly, trying to charm the station conductor into giving her a cheaper price.

"Sorry Miss, only first class tickets left," came the straight-faced reply. "We don't have cheap ones anymore."

"Please sir, my friend and I only have a little bit of money and we need to get a ticket to Myawaddy," she replied.

"Sorry Miss - that's the price, no money, no ride," the station inspector replied.

Thanda walked away annoyed.

"Urgh, *can you believe the nerve of that guy?*" she complained to Wunna. "Stiff won't give me a ticket!"

"Then we walk," he replied, calmly.

'What? Walk? I am in love with a crazy man! Walk? That's crazy talk. It's a long way to go!' she thought.

"You must be out of your mind! You want to leave this country as fast as you can, and you want to walk? It is going to take us months to reach Myawaddy! *We will be dead by then!*" she shrieked, attracting the stares of commuters.

Wunna shrugged. "We will find a way, Thanda. Do you trust me?"

His voice was all she needed to hear. It soothed her in a way she never expected. It was like he never understood the concept of anger.

'Was he dropped on his head when he was a child? Or does he just have a lot of patience?' she pondered.

She stormed off, shying away from the crowd of commuters, pacing herself in front of Wunna, with the suitcase in one hand and the orchids in the other.

He followed her, pacing himself behind her at a safe distance. He understood that she needed some time to let off some steam and she would have wanted some time alone. But her response baffled him. One moment she was assuring him that things were going to work out and the next, she was anxious. He was confused but he tried to remain calm and stay strong for the both of them.

'She must really want to get out of here too!' he thought. 'I know she trusts me, it's just - wow, I have never seen her so angry before!'

As Thanda walked away to try to calm herself down, the words, 'do you trust me?' resonated in Thanda's head. 'Okay, so the worst comes to worst, we walk, we can hitchhike, Wunna will find a way,' she resolved within herself.

'Wunna *will* find a way,' she reassured herself, stopping in her tracks. 'Wunna will find a way - yes! I do trust him! I must. He's the only one I have left.'

She turned around. As she saw him approaching in the near distance, she waited for him at where she stood. He caught up with her.

"I'm sorry Wunna, I shouldn't have reacted that way. I

do trust you," she said, placing the flowers in between

the suitcase handles and the suitcase on the sandy path.

"It's just that I'm scared. I want to make it out of here

too, with you. I don't want you to die. Staying here

longer only puts our lives in danger."

Wunna placed his palm on the side of her cheek. "It's

okay, we will make it through."

Hills and valleys.

Wunna and Thanda trekked along pathways in the rice fields. It took them about two to three days to reach another village, where they refuelled with rice and vegetables. Until then, Thanda, well versed with the harvests of the field, helped them to find food. Usually it was either fruits, or nuts, sometimes, honey.

There were times that Wunna questioned if running away was the right thing to do. He would be lost in thought. His mind replaying the events of that fateful night over and over again. There were times, when Thanda and him would be sleeping in sheds at night, and the nightmares of the killing would jolt him awake, drenching him in cold sweat.

They spent their days walking, talking, and resting under the shade of trees. Thanda's affection for Wunna had grown, so much more than before. She knew that at that time she wanted him, and now that they were together, her love grew for him, unconditionally. She understood the trauma he was facing. Sometimes, when they slept in the shed, she would, from the loft or whichever corner of the room she was sleeping in, see him struggling around in his sleep. She knew that it was his nightmares. She would comfort him the next day, telling him that it was okay, that all was going to be fine.

As days grew by, Thanda had gotten exhausted from all the walking, but the sights they saw together amazed her - how the hills and valleys worked hand in hand to form such scenic views. She noticed that Wunna started to look better as his hair grew out. She blushed at the thought.

'It's not all about his looks, but they do play an important part.' she reasoned within herself, feeling shy of her own affections towards Wunna.

***

One sunny afternoon, close to a month on foot, the two of them had reached a backwater area of the basin of the Sittaung River. They were in the region closer to the east side of Myanmar. Which meant that they were a few towns away from the border of Thailand.

They had made it closer.

"We are finally here!" exclaimed Thanda. "We are not far from Thailand."

"We have to cross this river," said Wunna.

"Hmm…I know! We'll just have to hop on a boat. I suppose we will have to wait for a fisherman or someone we can pay to cross the river!" came the reply.

"We just have to wait, I guess."

The weather was awfully hot that afternoon. As the two of them took refuge under the trees, Thanda had intended to go into the water. The thought of the feeling of the cool water on her skin excited her. She got up and walked slowly, barefoot through the grassy riverbank. She felt the water trickle through her toes. It was cool, offering comfort on this hot day. She turned around, looking at Wunna. He was resting under the tree, his eyes closed. The bark of the tree offered him a place for his head.

"Wunna!" she yelled. He opened his eyes and saw Thanda sitting by the bank of the river. Her *sarong* was soaked in water. She was smiling. "Come on! The water is perfect!" She motioned him to come.

So, he did. Rolling the legs of his jeans, he put his feet in the water. It was a nice feeling. Thanda scooped some water, cupping the palm of her hands and splashed some water on his face. Wunna winced at the coldness of the water, making her laugh at his reaction. He decided that it was time for revenge, in a playful way, of course. He stooped lower and scooped water, pouring it down Thanda's back.

"Oh, so that's how you want to play it, huh? You got it!" Thanda stood up and splashed more water on him.

They were playing like little kids for a while until they were soaked to the skin, their clothes sticking to their bodies as they made their way back to the river bank. They laughed as they fell back on the ground. Side by side they lay, looking up at the sky. Wunna was dizzy with happiness, and being next to Thanda, was all he needed to keep him from being overwhelmed and anxious about the events that had transpired. His mind drifted to the coin, in the excitement of jumping into the river, he suddenly feared that he would have dropped it. He didn't want to lose something so precious and valuable to him. He was reminded that there was some goodness in the world and forgiveness for him. In an attempt to quell his anxiety, he quickly checked the side pocket of his jeans for the coin, and he was relieved to find that it was still there safely tucked. He reflected on how the coin had brought him good fortune, but having Thanda by his side was good luck enough. He eyed Thanda, who was still gazing up at the sky, watching the cloud formations pass by.

Wunna heard the sound of rustling through the clearing.

"Thanda," he gently woke her.

She got up, snapping out of her reverie, "What is it?" she asked.

"Shhh," he placed a finger over his lips.

"What is it?" she whispered.

"I hear something," he mouthed, pointing to his ears.

More rustling. His heart pounded, a drumming sound in his ears. Thanda walked in front of Wunna. He held her hand reflexively, like how a child holds on to his mother's hand when he's scared.

"Don't be afraid," she said.

They moved to a corner behind the *lalang* plants that provided them a small hiding spot. From their hiding place, they saw an elderly man, struggling to drag a

rattan boat through the grassy clearing.

"Hey!" Thanda stood up, shouting and waving in his

direction. "Hey! Old man!"

The old man stopped whatever he was doing and

jumped up, startled. Wunna shot her a confused glance.

"Hey old man! Could you help us get across to the

other side?" Thanda yelled as she ran towards him.

"Could...could you help us?" She panted, pointing over

to the land that lay across the river.

Wunna ran after her.
"We have money, all you need to help us is to cross

over," said Thanda. "Please?" she added.

The old man nodded.

"I'm sorry if she startled you, sir," said Wunna.

The old man smiled and nodded his head. He pointed to his boat, gesticulating that it was stuck in the grassy clearing.

'He can't talk,' Wunna thought.

He ran over to the boat, seeing that it was stuck between some overgrown roots. The old man followed him.

"Wunna, is everything okay?" asked Thanda.

"The boat's stuck in the clearing. I am going to help him get this out, so we can go on our way," Wunna replied.

Wunna spent some time trying to get the boat out of the clearing. The old man watched him and helped. Wunna insisted he rest, for he looked frail.

'It's a wonder how he dragged the boat through to the river! Poor man,' he thought.

After what seemed like an eternity of fumbling about with the boat, Wunna managed to get the boat free. He then gave it one hard push and managed to get the boat into the water. The old man bowed his head as a sign of gratitude. Wunna reciprocated the gesture. Thanda grabbed the suitcase and hopped on to the boat. The old man got on it too. Wunna was the last one to get on it. He looked at the riverbank one more time, thanking God that they were on their way. The old man took an oar and rowed the boat, gently down the river, to the other side. When they reached, Thanda took out some money from the pocket of her blouse, to pay the old man. The old man refused to accept the money, even though they insisted. With the little they had, they wanted to bless the old man, as he had taken time off from fishing for his livelihood.

"Please, take it!" Thanda insisted, thrusting the money onto his palms.

The old man pointed to the other side of the river, the side they were initially on.

"Are you repaying us with a free ride because Wunna helped you get the boat out of those roots?" Thanda asked.

The old man nodded.

He mouthed the words, 'Thank you'.

"Thank you for your kindness, helping you was nothing, really," Wunna added. "In fact, you have blessed us more than we have."

The old man smiled and nodded. Wunna got out of the boat first, and helped Thanda out of it. The old man waved goodbye. They walked into another grassy clearing on the side of the riverbank. Wunna was holding the suitcase in one hand, and Thanda's hand in the other. As they walked, Thanda turned around, seeing the old man looking at them with vivacity in his eyes, smiling at her, and mouthing the words, 'Good luck.' She nodded, turned back and walked hand in hand with Wunna.

They trekked through miles of forests for a couple of hours before finding a small village. The day was starting to come to an end. The two of them were walking through a dimly lit village in the south western side of the town. They were hungry and were feeling cold as their clothes were still damp from their time at the riverbank in the afternoon.

As they walked through some street side food stalls, the scent of bamboo shoots and lemongrass filled the air. There was a man making stir-fried noodles with a portable gas stove from an extension at the back of his bike. The smell wafted through the air, making Thanda's and Wunna's mouth water in delight. They decided to stop by that stall and order some vegetarian rice noodles. The tasty, hot meal was absolutely fulfilling. After dinner, they walked towards the empty fields to rest for the evening. It had grown dark, except for the light of the stars that illuminated the night.

Thanda looked up and saw that the clear sky was just full of stars. She stopped in her tracks.

"Wunna, look!" Thanda gasped.

He looked up.

His eyes widened in amazement as he beheld the beauty nature had given them. Thanda lay down on the empty plain, eyes fixated on the stars. Wunna set the suitcase down, lying beside Thanda. He slid his hand into hers. She turned to look at him. He was looking intently, at the sky, in awe. It was the first time he had shown signs of affection, in the physical sense.

"Thanda! Look!" his voice, breaking her thoughts.

She shifted her focus back to the sky. They saw a shooting star.

"Wow," he exhaled.

Gold Coin

'As cliché as this whole thing is, it's sweet,' Thanda

mused as she felt a small smile creeping across her face.

She leaned closer to him, her head closer to his chest,

as they watched the stars in all their beauty.

'I'm never going to forget this day,' Thanda thought.

Cherishing the moment in her heart, she closed her

eyes and fell into a deep sleep.

Words.

Wunna woke up to the sounds of birds chirping. It was a somewhat cool morning as a light fog settled on the grassy plain. He opened his eyes, only to find the light of the morning sun jarring. He blinked several times to get the sun out of his eyes. He turned over to Thanda, only to find her leaning on his shoulder. She was fast asleep, her eyes shut, her breathing labored. Her hair covered part of her face. As if, almost naturally, he slipped his hand on her face, resting his palm on her cheek. He gently brushed the hair off her soft face. Her eyelids fluttered open. She looked at him and smiled.

"Morning," she said softly.

"Morning, my love," he whispered.

Waking up to such a response from Wunna came as a surprise to Thanda. It was a pleasant surprise. It was more than she could imagine.

***

It was another unusually hot afternoon. After trekking through rice fields, for what seemed like hours, the two of them decided to take some rest under a tree. Thanda found her spot between the exposed roots of the tree. She wedged herself in-between and placed the suitcase next to her. Wunna sat next to her, leaning back on the bark of the tree. Thanda fished out a thick, but compact black book. She opened it to the chapter where her bookmark lay.

Wunna saw what she was doing and looked at her. With an animated look on his face, he asked her, "What are you reading?"

"Oh, it's only the best book ever!" She replied. He extended his hand out, as if to take a look at it. She handed it to him.

He felt the weight of the book on his hands. He had never seen a written work like this. It felt rich and royal as it had a leather-bound cover. Thumbing through the pages he noticed the words were written in something cryptic; something he could never understand. He could not comprehend the fact that Thanda could take on a book like this. With small words and columns, with words no one could ever read.

"Here," he handed the book back to her. She took it from him. "Would you like me to read it to you?" she asked him.

"Are you going to read it to me in the language it was written in?" he quizzed.

"Of course not, silly! I will translate it to you," she replied.

"What language is this book written in?" Wunna asked.

"In English. This is really my favourite book. Would you like to hear a story?"

"Please, I would love to."

So, she started.

***

They spent more and more of their days trekking through small towns. With the little money they had, they made their way down to the Thai border. They

finally came close.

One particular afternoon, the rain was pouring down

hard. They were both soaked to the bone, cold and

desperate to find shelter. Eventually, Wunna and

Thanda found one in a street stall of a nearby village.

They both settled for a hot cup of tea. Sipping it slowly,

in drenched clothing, Wunna fished out the coin from

his pocket. He thumbed it in between his fingers and

tried to read what was written on it.

'What is it about this coin that has brought me good

luck?' he pondered.

Staring intently at the coin, his mind drifted to the old

lady, the things she had said, and the forgiveness she

extended to him. Thanda observed him as he was in a

trance with the coin. With her palms cupped around

the tin teacup, she brought the cup close to her lips,

sipping the tea as she turned her head gently to watch

the rain droplets pelt heavily from the aluminium roof

of the shop to the muddy ground. There was

something relaxing about watching the rain, the

experience of peace even in turmoil. She knew the

amount of pressure Wunna was in - running away from

who he was, finding himself only recently, and still,

beginning to love her in a way no one ever could.

"Thanda?" his voice interrupted her trail of thoughts.
She turned away from the rain and looked up at him.

"Thanda, do you think a coin can be lucky?" he leaned
over and handed the coin to her. She thumbed the
cool, gold coin and looked at it intently.

"Hmmm, I don't know. But whatever it is, if this coin makes you happy, then what's the point of thinking about its value? It already means something to you."

Wunna paused for a moment, contemplating what Thanda had said.

"I guess you're right. This coin does mean something to me. May this coin always serve as a reminder for me to do good, to forgive and to love," he replied, with his mind reeling to the old woman; to Thanda following him on this journey; and to the days where he felt blessed with her presence.

Walk.

The journey to Thailand had finally come to an end. Darkness enveloped their surroundings, except for some fireflies that illuminated the night sky. There were no signboards, no people, no border security officers. They made their way across the road and into some paddy fields. They used the light from the fireflies as a guide through the night. A few minutes short of the sunrise, Wunna and Thanda found a place to rest.

"We made it," Wunna heaved, relieved.

"Finally," Thanda exhaled and blinked, resting her head on the bark of the tree they were seated under. They watched the sun rise in its glorious shade of gold and orange.

***

Wunna and Thanda made their way through a small town in the Thai side of the border.

"I am actually really hungry," Thanda said. "So hungry, I could eat a cow!"

Wunna winced at the thought of hurting the poor animal, "you're actually going to eat a whole cow?"

Thanda laughed, "not a whole cow. Maybe not even a part of it!" Thanda exclaimed. "It's just an expression that you say, when you're very hungry," she explained.

"I'm hungry too, but all my life I've been vegetarian," came the innocent reply.

"So maybe, you're so hungry, you could eat a whole rice field?" Thanda joked.

The two of them laughed as they made their way to a small food stall for lunch.

That afternoon, the two of them walked through the small provincial town. It was a pretty busy and nominally warm afternoon, with a lot of hustle and bustle in the streets.

Elderly ladies with straw hats were seated along the pavements, drinking tea off of tin cups; young kids and their mothers walking out of the nearby primary school and old men pushing carts with fresh tropical fruits.

***

It had been a week since Wunna and Thanda had made their home in the small border town in Thailand. They had some money from their journey and they decided to stay in a small apartment complex. Thanda was, according to Wunna, resourceful enough to get the money changed – from *Kyats* to *Baht*. As Thanda knew some basic Thai, she was able to converse with some of the locals to assist with their needs. Coupled with the money she had changed, and the fierce negotiations that Thanda had with the apartment manager, they found a cheap room in a 3-storey apartment complex to rent.

It was a single-unit apartment, with shower facilities located outside, shared by all the residents living on the same floor as them, and some mats provided for them to sleep on. The second floor apartment faced the busy street and by day it was very dusty and humid, but at night, it provided a refuge from the light rain droplets that pelted from the heavens.

One afternoon, as Thanda was on her way out of a sundry shop, she saw a poster in English, advertising for a teaching job. *'Be an English teacher today! Change the lives of many people!'* the poster read. There were contact details on the poster and this had piqued her interest. Thanda felt that she had hit the jackpot, as she was educated in the English language by her father. She knew grammar, and she was an avid reader, always having a dictionary by her side to aid her when she faced unfamiliar words. She became excited about the prospect of being employed.

'Plus, I'll be earning an income!' she contemplated. 'I really don't see how this will be a problem. I can work enough so that we can move to a better place. We can have a better life together!' She hurriedly walked back to her apartment.

She ran up the flight of stairs, panting, heaving as she opened the door. In her excitement, she dropped her sundries on the floor with a loud bang, announcing her entrance to Wunna, who was sprawled on his man, enjoying his siesta. Hearing the loud noise, Wunna jolted awake from his afternoon nap. Propping himself up on his elbows, he squinted his eyes, blinking slowly to orientate himself.

"Thanda, what is it?" he asked.

"I just saw an ad for a job. I think I may know how to get us out of here," she replied. "But the only thing that's holding me back is the fact that we are not even citizens of Thailand."

"Hey Wunna, what do you think if we get registered as citizens of Thailand?" Thanda asked.

"Thanda, if I get registered, won't they find me? I'm a criminal, a murderer. It would be my head they would look for!" Wunna exclaimed. "This is a ridiculous idea, Thanda! We *cannot* go through with this."

He turned his face away from Thanda and looked towards the only window that illuminated their apartment.

Thanda walked over to Wunna's mat where he rested and gently grabbed both his hands,

"Look at me, Wunna," she demanded, locking her gaze onto his face. "Wunna, *we have the opportunity to reinvent ourselves here*," Thanda shrieked.

"WOULD YOU KEEP YOUR VOLUME DOWN IN THERE!" an irritated voice boomed from outside their room.

Wunna looked at Thanda in shock. He was still quite dazed from his nap and he didn't take it too kindly that Thanda had reacted this way. While he understood what she was trying to say, he was afraid that the consequences of his actions would come to find him in the most horrible way possible. He was scared and he just wanted to protect himself, and now, Thanda. He tried to keep is composure as Thanda slowly moved closer to him. Thanda reduced her monologue to a fine whisper, inching close to Wunna's face.

"Look, no one know us, except for the innkeeper – that too, he only knows us as that loud girl and her soft-spoken friend. Come on Wunna, take a chance on me. You trust me, *and* you love me – and I do too. But we need to get registered as citizens so that I can get a job and maybe – you could try one too. We can earn money and be able to afford to keep this apartment.

We can, maybe even, save enough money to find a better place for us to live in. We can put our past behind us and be the people we want to be. Don't you see that?"

"I'll have to think about this Thanda," came the feeble reply. "I'm scared. Even after all that's happened – I still have blood on my hands."

Beginnings.

A flash of light enveloped the room. Wunna was seated in front of a white tarp in an old photo studio in the town.

"Next!" yelled the old, balding man behind the camera. He was rather plump and held a cigarette between the fingers of his free hand, the other on the camera. He seemed impatient and wanted to get his job over and done with.

Thanda adjusted her hair and the cotton blouse she was wearing. She pulled her fringe away from her eyes as she made her way to the seat.

"I don't have all day, missy," said the old man, as he took a drag of his cigarette.

"C'mon, I just want to look good for my picture!" Thanda replied.

The shopkeeper grunted and took her picture.

It was truly a wonder how Thanda convinced Wunna to register for Thai citizenship. Wunna had taken a lot of time to think about it. Firstly, the money that they had taken at the beginning of the journey, although they were frugal in their spending, was fast running out. He knew that one of them needed to get a job to address the issue of finances. And to get a job, they had to be citizens. Especially for Thanda, as she wanted to teach English in the village's school. Secondly, the thought of reinventing themselves – becoming new people, resonated very much with Wunna. He kept going back to the "murder", the old lady, and the coin. He remembered Thanda telling him, once, during the journey, that the coin was a reminder of forgiveness

that the old lady had shown him. He had spent
sleepless nights thinking and pondering on these two
things.

One night, while Wunna laid on his mat, he began
deliberating. He took the coin out from the makeshift
necklace that cradled the coin and he stared at it. And
his mind reeled back to the night that changed
everything.

"I have been running for so long. But what exactly am
I running away from? The lady has forgiven me. I am a
free man, so why am I running?" he muttered under his
breath.

'Maybe it's time for you to come home,' said a small
voice in his head. 'This is your life now. Isn't this what
you wanted?'

He looked over to his left, where Thanda was fast asleep. She was sleeping on the other side of the room, on a straw mat with a thin blanket draped over her shoulders. She was snoring softly, deeply asleep, without a care in the world – or so it seemed, to Wunna.

He turned and shifted his focus back to the coin. He could hear the sound of a light drizzle outside the apartment window. He closed his eyes and inhaled deeply.

'Yes, this is what I wanted. Just not the way I expected it to be,' he murmured in reply.

Days grew into months, and the seasonal monsoon rains seemed to fall hard in the small provincial town that they had lived in. Thanda and Wunna had both collected their reinvented Thai identities from the local government office. Thanda had managed to land the

job at a Christian organization that aimed at equipping
the locals with the Basic English Language, so that they
could get better job opportunities and be able to
adequately provide for their families. Thanda was paid
a decent salary, and that helped to cover their expenses.
They were not big spenders and hence, they were able
to save some money for themselves to start their new
lives in Thailand.

As Thanda was working to provide for the two of
them, Wunna had to learn the art of cooking and
overseeing household responsibilities, such as getting
the groceries that mostly consisted of vegetables and
rice, and cleaning the house. Wunna also learnt how to
cook quick and simple meals, as Thanda had taught
him over the weekends, when she wasn't working.

The couple had grown accustomed to their lifestyle,
living under one roof as friends. During their months

in the house, Wunna had opened-up a lot of his life to Thanda. He told her stories of his time spent in the monastery, his friends, how he missed his teacher – his one and only parent, the man he could call his father, but didn't. He opened up about that fateful night that caused him to have nightmares every time he saw those eyes of fearlessness in the man he killed, and the forgiveness of a woman – so great, the human mind could not comprehend. And even if it did, it would cause the smartest of men to question humanity.

One humid January afternoon, as Wunna was in the nearby sundry shop getting some provisions for the house, he heard a clamor outside. He quickly paid the shopkeeper and collected his items. With a plastic bag in hand, he ran outside to see what the buzz was all about. He saw people running towards the statue of Buddha, which stood at the roundabout of the main street in that town, and throwing stones at it. He was stupefied when he saw what was happening.

'Blasphemy! These people are traitors to the God they worship!' he thought.

To him, this was truly an abomination. As he made his way towards the protesters, he saw a man he recognized as the photographer who helped him and Thanda with the photos they had to take.

Wunna stopped him and asked, "Sir, what is going on? Why are these people blaspheming the God they worship?"

"They are not like us, they don't believe what we believe in," the photographer said. "Those people, always rallying our people to their side, destroying everything we believe in," he continued, bitterly.

"We should stop them and find out why they are doing it," Wunna replied.

"What's the use, kid? They are beyond reason. They are violent," came the reply.

Wunna ran towards the crowd and blended in as he saw a man, with a loudhailer, approached the pedestal that encapsulated the Buddha statue and stood in front of it. As the stoning of the statue had stopped, that man's silhouette became clearer. Wunna saw the man for who he was. A liar. In his heart, he knew that Islam meant love. The teachings of the *Quran* had the all-encompassing message of love. It was that love and mercy that the old Muslim woman showed to him, forgiving him and telling him to live.

He knew that if Islam preached hate, he would not have been standing at where he was.

Clad in black, a bearded man stood in front of the statue. Pressing the loudhailer to his lips, he started, "Ladies and gentlemen, boys and girls, we of the brotherhood are here to tell you that you are wrong. We will fight against the infidels. We will take your streets. We will become the gods you will soon worship. If you are Muslim and you believe everything I tell you, we will fight against the infidels of this country. This will be ours!" he cheered.

There were some roars coming from the crowd. Some cheers amidst the general fear that the rest of the people resonated. Wunna was afraid but he kept silent.

'This isn't real! They're all liars!' the voice in his mind rang.

With quiet confidence, the man in the black tunic continued to push his tirade. "Only those who are serious about joining our cause can join. You must give up everything you know, your friends and family, although it's going to be difficult, you must pick up your arms and fight with us, for us, for the sake of the brotherhood for we are the chosen ones."

More roars from a few men in the crowd.

"So, join our-" he stopped short, as a loud cry emerged from the back of the crowd.

"*LIAR!* YOU'RE A LIAR!" A man, dressed exactly like the man in black - except that he was older, and clad in a white garment, walked towards the crowd. The crowd made way for him as he made his way to the pedestal, where the man in black was standing.

"This is not what *Allah* preached. We are to love our neighbors. We were called to extend love and forgiveness to the people around us. *You are a liar!*" the man in the white tunic rebuked the man spewing hate.

"You're just a coward," the man replied smugly. "Too afraid to fight for what you and I both know is true."

"If it is, truly, you would not be sowing this discord among our brethren. You, in your so-called position of authority, would learn to love others," the man dressed in white replied.

Turning to the crowd, the older man pointed to the man with the loudhailer saying, "this man is a liar, anyone who wants to follow him, you can. But all I can say is that you're just going to be walking to your death."

Walking away, the older man felt a sense of pride for standing up for what he believed to be true. He wanted all to love one another. He knew that in order for everyone to co-exist peacefully, it had to stem from that special, unconditional love that came from above.

The man with the loudhailer seemed visibly uncomfortable with what the older man had just said. As the older man in the white garment walked away, the man in the black tunic regained his composure, pressed his loudhailer to his lips and continued to speak convincingly to the crowd. Wunna made his way out of the crowd and sprinted after the man in white.

"Hey, wait up!" Wunna panted. The older man stopped to turn. "I saw you back there. And I have to say, I entirely agree with you."

"Hi..er..," the older man paused, surprised at this random interaction.

The two men walked along the sandy pavement. Wunna with a plastic bag of groceries in his hand and the other with a heart on his sleeve. "What you said back there, I totally agree" Wunna said, supportively.

"You do?" the man replied.

"Yes, you were right in what you said, sir," Wunna replied. "Good luck stopping your brother. I sincerely hope he changes his mind."

"You sound like you've experienced this before," the older man commented.

"You seem like a good man, sir. It has, in fact, happened to me before, but it went bad. I didn't want any part in it, but it happened. I was caught in the middle because I couldn't change my brother's mind," Wunna explained.

"No matter how hard you tried?" The man questioned.

Wunna nodded. "But I gave up on my brother. He was incorrigible. But because of what happened, I now know peace. And forgiveness."

He toyed with the coin around his neck.

"I wish you all the best, sir, don't give up. God knows you are trying and your brother is not you," Wunna commented.

The man nodded in agreement. He felt a sense of peace from Wunna's words of affirmation.

"My friend, I think there is a reason why we crossed paths today. God knows that I have been upset and I want to stop whatever that has been happening. You have encouraged me, brother," the older man said as he shook Wunna's hand.

Wunna nodded, thanking the man for standing up for truth as they exchanged their goodbyes.

***

That evening, Wunna breathlessly recounted the entire incident with the man in white and the man in black to Thanda. She was startled at first, but she listened.

"So that's what happened just now! My goodness! It was scary! But I hope he managed to talk that guy out of whatever he's doing," said Wunna.

"I do hope so too, but if the man in black is hateful as you say he is, what if he plans to do something to hurt this community?" Thanda replied. She was anxious. "I don't want to lose you, Wunna. We've come so far, and maybe it's time for us to get to a safe place, away from here, perhaps."

"But Thanda, there are good people too! Look at the older man - my friend, for instance, he's trying to do something by stopping it from happening."

"Do you really think he's going to be able to talk that man out? I mean it could have made him even more angry."

"I hope he will be able to get through to the troublemaker."

"Yeah," she scoffed, stopping him short, "Just like how it went with you and Thiha?"

Wunna snapped. He felt a pang of anger hit him in the gut and the frustration he had was like a blood-rush to the head. He knew that this topic was something he was still traumatized about and he never expected Thanda to use that against him. He felt angry for the first time in a long time. But he knew the best way forward was to remain calm and not shout at Thanda. Closing his eyes and taking a deep breath, he tried to nonchalantly walk out of the house, but he slammed the ratty main door of the apartment in his anger. Thanda was startled. She had never seen Wunna so angry before. The fact that he slammed the door was news to her. She knew that she had hit a nerve. She stared at the noodles she prepared for dinner, sipped some water from a tin cup and tried to fight back her tears. She chewed the lower part of her lip, but she couldn't help it, she wept. Burying her face in her hands, she leaned on the table, until she fell asleep.

Wunna was walking on the dusty pavement that ran along the street they lived in. Around him, the sun was setting, shops were closing, and the light of the fireflies were beginning to envelop the near empty street. It was a mildly warm evening.

He wanted to move on. This reminder was just a slap in his face. In the back of his mind, he knew that Thanda was right. He had, too, tried the same thing all those months ago, to convince his brother not to incite hatred against others. In an odd sense, he knew that the older man wasn't going to be successful in talking to the man with the loudhailer– to tell him to stop. The man had already made up his mind - to destroy anyone he felt was an infidel.

He was just afraid to admit to Thanda that the older man might fail. He still wanted to believe that there could be some good that might come out from this situation. He felt that there could have been some peace, but he knew that it was unattainable. He was too much of a dreamer, an idealist.

He walked to the end of the street, and on to the next lane.

It was in times like these, he was reminded of his teacher, U Chin. When he was alive, he remembered how he taught Wunna important lessons on co-existing with people of different religious beliefs. He was always telling Wunna that peace and harmony made society work.

'It is pride that blinds us,' Wunna remembered his mentor's words.

It was true, people just wanted to be right, just wanted the power that came from being right. Saying that they have found God and killing others in that name gave great power to the person executing it.

'In that sense, I have also been blinded by pride. I just wanted Thanda to be wrong about this' he mused. 'I was wrong.' He stopped in his tracks.

By now, the sky had grown from a pleasant shade of pink to a dark blue. He looked up and saw the vastness of the sky. The velvet hues of the dark blue and black, just illuminated with the billions of stars that hung in the balance of nothingness. He took a deep breath and marveled at the beauty of the sky. For some reason, musing over nature's wonders gave him a sense of peace. He looked down at his dusty feet and felt so small.

He remembered what Thanda read to him when they were on their journey. She said that there was a being, called God. According to her book, this God spoke and the earth, the sky and the universe was formed.

'This God must have good taste, making the sky so beautiful like that,' he marveled.

It was, for some reason, a comforting thought.

When he got home, he saw Thanda asleep on the floor next to the round and short dinner table. The dinner she had prepared was cold. There were a few small flies swarming around the food. He looked at her and he saw that she had been crying. Her eyes were swollen and red.

He gently placed his hand on her shoulder and whispered, "I'm so sorry Thanda. I was wrong, *I* was so wrong."

He placed a mat in the middle of the room where she usually slept and carried her to the mat. He lay her down gently and placed a soft pillow. She stirred, but she fell back asleep. He cleared the uneaten meal and cleaned the place. Just before he fell asleep, he began to meditate, pondering over the sense of calm he received from looking at the night sky and the God, the Creator of those stars Thanda spoke about, and fell into a deep sleep.

Reconciliation.

When Thanda awoke the next morning, she had to re-orientate her surroundings. She was on her sleeping mat and her pillow. The last thing she remembered was sitting on the floor and placing her hands on the table and crying. She sat up and looked for Wunna. He wasn't in their small apartment.

'Did he even come home last night?' she wondered.

His mat and pillow were rolled up, and left at the side of the room, as he usually kept it. She got up, and rolled her mat and placed her pillow atop the mat. She saw that the dinner table had been cleared.

'He must have come home,' she mused.

It was a comforting thought. She took her towel and some clothes from a dresser and her toothbrush and toothpaste from the top of the dresser. She walked into the shared bathroom at the end of the hallway.

It wasn't long before she heard a loud bang, infernal screams followed by another loud bang. Panic enveloped her soul, she quickly got dressed and ran out of the bathroom. The manager of the apartment complex saw her coming out of the bathroom. He quickly pulled her to the lone window at the other end of the hallway and what she saw was nothing short of pandemonium in the street. She felt a tightening in her chest.

People were running around everywhere. Smoke enveloped the air. There was blood smeared along the dusty street. There were overturned fruit carts. There were people covered in blood. Children, men and women crying, weeping over their dead loved ones and their injuries. The sound of ambulance sirens blaring at a distance. Thanda shut her eyes and started to cry. She thought of Wunna and the fight. She was so afraid for his safety.

'What if he's dead?' She panicked at the thought.

The sounds around her faded away as she began to feel lightheaded. The apartment manager held on to her and made her sit on the floor. He pulled her close to him and told her that everything was going to be okay.

"Wunna, Wunna…" her voice trailed off.

She tried to break free from the apartment manager, but she began to black out.

"Wake up," The apartment manager lightly tapped her shoulder. "We'll go downstairs and talk to the police, I can hear them coming. We can ask them about your boyfriend okay?"

He slung her arm over his shoulder and lifted her to the front desk of the apartment, which was two flights of stairs down. She weakly hobbled on. When they were at the front desk, he took a bottle of water and fed it to her. When he saw that she was steady, the apartment manager ran out into the street and asked a nearby police officer to help him with Thanda. The young police officer, escorted by the apartment manager, rushed into the dilapidated inn. Thanda was slumped over the counter.

The manager woke her up, and with a lot of concern in his voice, he said, "this man can help you."

The police officer acknowledged the apartment manager.

Thanda looked at the police officer. "Can you help me find him?"

"How is he related to you, miss?" the police officer asked.

"He's my friend. Is he…"

"Dead?" the officer finished her sentence. "I don't know. But why don't you come down to the hospital with me?"

Tearing up, she asked, "He'll be there?"

"Everyone who was either dead or injured was brought there," came the reply from the police officer.

Thanda nodded. The young police officer escorted her out to his patrol jeep and headed for the hospital. When they arrived at the hospital, they had to go around through the back entrance. It wasn't a very big hospital. It was a three-storey building, slightly dilapidated with moss and mildew growing out at the sides of the building. They walked in through the open hallway of the back entrance. It was narrow and the steady low buzz of the overhead lights hummed through the dimly lit hallway. The police officer walked as Thanda followed suit. It was a quiet entryway as compared to the one in front. A faint sting of disinfectant lingered in the air. And the surrounding area was cold.

As Thanda walked along the hallway, she noticed the sign above a door that read 'Mortuary'. She shuddered at the thought of finding Wunna there. Naturally, she clasped her palm over her mouth, attempting to muffle her cries. The police officer turned around, hearing soft, muffled whimpering.

When he saw her crying, he said to her, "don't cry, Miss. We will find him."

She wasn't assured. She wanted to see Wunna, to hold him and to tell him that everything was going to be okay. The police officer led Thanda to the main reception wing of the hospital. There was a sense of panic and urgency that filled the air. The rush of the nurses and doctors, running around with stretchers, people crying and screaming from both emotional and physical pain, and the ringing of phones in the main reception lobby, just elevated the pressure for Thanda. She was desperate to know if he was alive. There, they inquired about the victims of the blast.

"We are looking for a man, in his early to mid 20s," the police officer started. Pointing to Thanda, he added, "this is his friend, she is very worried for him."

The police officer, who didn't want Thanda to get more worried, asked the receptionist, "Where are the injured?"

"They are in the ward upstairs, ward 26," replied the nurse. Then looking at Thanda, "I hope you find your friend."

Both Thanda and the police officer made their way towards the closed stairwell at the side of the reception lobby. They ran up the stairs, and opened the door to the second floor. The hallways outside the wards were filled with people, anxious, looking for their loved ones. Thanda and the police officer made their way carefully around them, heading towards the ward.

When Thanda stepped into the ward, she saw the shopkeeper's wife, from the provision shop they used to get their groceries from. The shopkeeper's wife immediately recognized her and ran towards her. They hugged and wept over the fear that they may have lost their loved ones even as the police officer tried to calm them down and escort them into the ward. They saw the shopkeeper first, who was seated on a wooden chair, with a bandage over his right eye. His disposition was one mangled with shock, fear and pain. The shopkeeper's wife led out a shrill cry as she ran to him and held him, thanking God that he was alive. Thanda was hoping, just like the shopkeeper's wife, that she too would find Wunna alive.

'Thanda,' she heard a whisper. Someone called out to her. It sounded like Wunna.

Instinctively, she turned around. There was no one she knew around her, just strangers, fearful, heightened, panicked, some looking for their loved ones, and others hugging them, weeping.

'Wunna?' She responded, also with a whisper.

'Thanda, can you see me?'

'Thanda!'

She woke up.

***

Jolted awake, all she could hear was a soft breathing of someone else in the apartment.

Soft rays of sunlight seeped through the dusty wooden framed window, casting a glimmer on Wunna. Thanda wiped the sleep from her eyes and propped herself up on her mat. She gently brushed the hair out of her eyes with her hands, tying all the loose strands into a neat bun, and began to get up. She rolled her mat back to where she had usually kept it, in a corner between the window and the small mirror that was framed on the wall.

She noticed that the apartment was immaculately clean, the food from last night cleared, the dishes washed and the small table wiped, and the floor swept. She took her towel and her clothes from the ratty chest of drawers that held both their attire. At the top of the chest were her toiletries. She retrieved them and headed to the external shared bathroom at the end of the walkway of the apartment complex to freshen up.

Her mind was still reeling from the unpleasant exchange with Wunna and the dream that she had, occupying her thoughts as she took a shower. Deliberating her fear of losing him and Wunna's desires of helping his new-found friend, she felt that her fears were selfish. She loved him, and she had known it for a long time. He was broken when he came to her that night, and all through their journey, he had shared his regrets and she felt his pain of losing his teacher, and his brothers, whom he thought he could have saved. He wanted to help his new-found friend desperately so that he could find some sort of redemption for himself.

But she feared losing him, in the event that if he tried to help his new-found friend and died in the process.

'Will he ever know how much I love him?' she pondered.

She tried to push the thought away.

'A safe place is what we need, yet, protecting him is selfish.'

'I have to stay!'

'What if I lose him?'

Recurring thoughts like this made her want to cry. She wanted desperately to be with him, but she also wanted him to feel a sense of accomplishment, at least, so that he could say that he tried.

When she returned, she saw that Wunna was still fast asleep. She placed her towel and her hand-washed clothes to dry on the drying rack. Walking over to the chest, she retrieved her comb and brushed her wet hair. Finding the small round tin of sandalwood paste, she took a generous amount and applied it on her face and hands. She heard Wunna stirring as he got up from his slumber.

She turned to face him. "Wunna, I am so sorry about-"

"I'm sorry, Thanda. I shouldn't have gotten angry with you last night" Wunna apologized.

Thanda walked over to Wunna and sat beside him.

"I should have been more sensitive about what I said. I am afraid of losing you Wunna, but I don't want you to live in regret of the things you could do to right your wrongs," Thanda admitted.

He propped up from his mat and gently placed a finger over Thanda's lips, as if to silence her.

"Thanda, you were right, I was wrong. I let my fears get the best of me. I don't want to lose you too," he reassured.

He held her cheek in the palm of his hand. She rested, with tears rolling down her face. He leaned in and kissed her gently on her forehead.

"I love you."

"I love you, too."

Desires.

Wunna and Thanda had decided to get married in the late summer. There was no point rushing since they had known their love for each other, and it began to grow with every passing moment. Thanda had saved part of her earnings that month so that they could pay to get their marriage certificate and buy some nice clothes for their solemnization ceremony, even if it meant eating plain rice porridge and pickles for every meal.

It was a beautiful Saturday morning. The day was cloudless and blue and the sun was comfortably warm. Summer was almost over, and sneaks of seasonal rain had begun, albeit minimal. It was a day Thanda and Wunna had waited patiently for and one they would never forget – it was their wedding day. They proceeded to the local government office in the morning to register their marriage with the shopkeeper

and his wife as witnesses.

Thanda had sewn her own wedding dress - a light

crème coloured silk dress that held a simple boat

framed collar, seamed at the waist with a light flair

ending at the shin – which she spent a considerable

amount of time every night after dinner preparing. She

wore a simple black pair of shoes that she had bought

from the market and decorated her hair with the

flowers the florist had given her as a wedding gift when

she had found out that they were getting married.

Thanda held a small bouquet of purple and white

orchids. On that day, she looked stunning with the

dress accentuating every curve of her body. She seemed

to emanate some sort of light, making Wunna blush.

Clad in a fresh pair of black pants and a white shirt,

tucked into his pants, and a new pair of shoes, Thanda

was stunned at how fresh and flawless Wunna looked.
He had a new haircut which enhanced his features,
highlighting his high cheekbones. She blushed like a
schoolgirl, in awe and in admiration, of the man she
was going to marry.

The shopkeeper had bought a small camera, not out of
his own free will, but out of Thanda's pleas and the
promise that she was going to treat him and his wife to
a sumptuous lunch, all just to immortalize this
moment. The shopkeeper's wife was just very happy to
witness her favourite couple get married. They were
clad in their Sunday best, and the shopkeeper's wife
had a small silk handkerchief ready, as she knew that
she was going to cry.

The wedding ceremony was a simple one. All they had
to do was to place their thumb prints on the wedding
certificate to confirm their agreement to one another,

after they had exchanged their wows. The shopkeeper's

wife, predictably, cried with tears of joy for her beloved

friends as she and her husband looked on. The

ceremony ended within ten minutes. Wunna and

Thanda held hands for the first time as man and wife,

as they went for their wedding lunch with the

shopkeeper and his wife at a small roadside stall.

"Thank you so much for coming to our ceremony,"

Thanda said to the shopkeeper and his wife. "You guys

have been like second parents to us, especially to

Wunna," she said, winking playfully with a smile as she

looked at Wunna.

"Oh, honey, it was a pleasure! We are honoured to

have been invited to your wonderful ceremony! We

wish you all the best in your married life, sweetheart!"

The shopkeeper's wife exclaimed. "Don't we, hon?"

she nudged her husband.

The shopkeeper with his mouth stuffed in a bowl of noodles, looked up and grunted "huh", slurping his noodles and chewing them as quick as he could, "yes, yes. Lovely indeed. Please come to collect your photos on Tuesday, kids," he said dismissively, focusing on his food.

After the meal, they thanked the shopkeeper and his wife again for honouring them and headed back to their apartment, hand in hand as Husband and Wife.

***

Seasons had begun to change. Long gone were the days of blue skies and summer-seasonal fruits. The monsoon rains had begun, with heavy rains pelting hard throughout the nights. Thanda had still been teaching in the mission school while Wunna continued to help out around the house. Nothing had seemingly changed, except for the fact that Thanda was pregnant.

The day she found out she was pregnant, she was in complete awe and joy, knowing that this child was testament to the love she and Wunna had shared. She had only wished that Ming was with her to partake in the joy of becoming an uncle. She tried to call her brother several times in the past few months since she had lived in Thailand, but he never picked up the calls. She wondered if anything had happened to him, so she tried one more time from the phone booth outside the sundry shop – on the day she found out that she was pregnant.

Ming happened to be by the phone that day, apparently expecting a call from his friend who had been recruiting for the military in Myanmar.

He picked up on the third ring.

"Ming?"

"Thanda? How are you?!" He exclaimed.

"Ming! I miss you. I've been trying to call you for the past few months," she replied, dolefully.

"Oh, I see. I must have been out those few times! It's so good to hear from you," Ming replied.

"Me too, Ming. I miss you so much! I'm in Thailand now," Thanda informed.

"Across the border? It's good you left while you could. Things, uh, well, they are getting a little crazy around here."

"Crazy?" she quizzed.

"Yeah, a lot of talk about shutting down the country from outsiders," he replied with sadness in his voice. "I've been given a job with the military," he continued, quietly.

"Ming, does that mean I never get to see you again?"

"I don't know. But all you need to know is that I love you, always."

She teared up. Biting her lip and putting on a brave face, she replied, "oh, don't be so melodramatic Ming, we'll see each other sometime soon. At least I'll keep hoping till I see you again. Be safe."

Trying to fight back his tears, he replied, "You too, kid."

Their conversation had ended on a melancholic tone. She was happy to have finally spoken to her brother, whom she had adored all her life. But she had also known and heard stories about people recruited in the military, and how they had never come home. She never knew when she'd ever get to talk to him again. It was a bittersweet moment encapsulated in time, as she knew she would never get the chance to tell Ming about her baby.

***

A couple of months had passed since the phone call and Thanda was becoming irritable with each passing day. Her belly had swelled up and she was not getting good sleep at night. The mat was becoming uncomfortable for her as her back had been hurting, growing in its intensity. Wunna had no idea how to help her except to cook her favourite meals and give her the care she needed. They had been going for regular check-ups at the free clinic and the doctor had been so kind as to give additional advice to help them prepare for the birth of their baby.

***

A short sharp pain seared through Thanda's back and belly. 'It's happening! It's really happening,' she thought to herself.

It had been 8 months since the phone call to Ming.

Thanda was in the market when she felt the contractions again. She knew that the baby was going to come out soon and the contractions were coming on stronger and faster between each cycle, and when it came, it felt like someone was shooting her and pulling the bullet out, and then shooting her again.

Taking deep breaths, she walked briskly towards Wunna, who was buying vegetables from the shop nearby. The market was crowded and the chatter of bargain hunters swept through her yelps. She gripped through the pain, biting her teeth and clenching her fists as she made her way to tell her husband that she was finally having the baby.

"Wunna!" she called through gritted teeth, tapping him on the shoulder ferociously. "I think I'm having the baby."

"You think?" came the slightly confused reply.

"I *know*," she growled, in a half-whispering way. "I've been carrying this baby, of course I know!" she snapped.

"Okay, let's go to the hospital" came the feeble reply.

There were so many emotions that hit Wunna like a tidal wave. As he clutched Thanda's hand, they tried to walk as fast as they could to the hospital nearby. Whenever Thanda was in pain she would grip Wunna's hand a little tighter and scream a little. She would crouch down, clutching her belly before regaining her stupor and grabbing him by the hand and leading the way to the hospital.

"We are going to have this baby, we are going to have this baby, we are going to have this baby," she repeated in her head over and over again, as they were making their way to the hospital, which was, thankfully, only five minutes away from the market.

After what felt like an eternity, they finally made it to the hospital.

"She's having a baby!" Wunna exclaimed to the nurse at the front-desk. His voice filtered through excitement and anxiety.

"Okay, let me help you," a ward attendant said, bringing a wheelchair to Thanda, who was clutching her belly in pain. She let out a scream and the ward attendant motioned her to sit down on the wheelchair.

Wunna followed suit as the ward attendant wheeled her into the delivery ward. "You have to wait here," said the ward attendant, pointing to the rusting mint green chairs in the waiting room.

Wunna nodded and waited anxiously, holding on to Thanda's purse and a plastic bag full of vegetables. Staring at the paint peeling wall, he shifted his focus to the dusty window pane, hoping that the baby will come out healthy and happy. He was scared and worried for Thanda as he didn't want anything to happen to her. Fiddling with the coin he had hung around his neck all these years, he prayed for everything to be okay.

***

Loud cries began to fill the room. Beads of perspiration ran down Thanda's forehead and neck.

"Calm down!" said one of the nurses as she held Thanda's hand.

Thanda screamed again. Gripping the nurse's hand, she said, "I want to DIE! KILL ME NOW!"

"Just breathe in, and out, slowly darling," said the nurse. "Just keep breathing and listen to the sound of my voice okay?"

Thanda nodded.

The pain came once more and Thanda let out another blood-curdling scream.

"Okay, I think she is ready to give birth," said the nurse to the midwife. "Okay, now you need to push."

With all her might, she pushed.

"I still can't see anything!" yelled the nurse. "You need to push harder darling!"

Another push.

"How much longer?" Thanda screamed.

"I can see the head!" exclaimed the midwife.

"You need to push one more time darling, you can do this!" said the nurse.

'Please God, I hope this baby comes out,' Thanda thought.

One last push.

It was at that moment, the world felt still. Thanda's vision became blurry as she leaned back on the pillows. She let out one final scream.

Gold Coin

Out came a soft cry.

Redemption.

The waiting room was awfully quiet. For such a time as this, it was unusual. It had only been a few hours since they left the market to get to the hospital and it wasn't as if the waiting room was empty. There were people milling about the room, waiting – with bated breath, for their loved ones to come out of whatever room they were in. Although the room itself was filled with silence, there was hope, anxiety and anticipation that permeated the air. It just so happened that Wunna was one of them. His anxiety to see Thanda and their newborn was mangled with hope, fear and happiness.

'I am going to be a father!' he mused, anticipating how he would be to his child.

Was he going to be a good father? Was he going to be a strict father? Or was he going to pamper his child so much so that he could give him or her all the love and attention they deserved? Toying with the coin around his neck he said a soft prayer.

'Teacher, if only you could see me now, to see my child. Please give me the guidance to be a good father to my child, to love and to cherish my wife and to be grateful and caring to my family. I miss you and I hope to see you again,' he teared.

He shut his eyes, soaking in the silence of the room, hearing the soft hum of the fluorescent lights and the prominent ticking of the clock. Focusing his mind on the sound of the clock, he waited.

'Breathe, just breathe,' he mumbled to himself.

It was at that moment; the room began to shift. The soundscape had changed. He could hear sounds reminiscent of gunfire, at a distance, but not so far away. Packed with a sense of urgency, he opened his eyes and ran towards the window to see what was going on.

It was chaos.

There were people running in all directions. Babies crying – people shrieking at the sight of bloodshed. Rusty black and tinted vans were approaching in all directions surrounding the hospital. A stream of men, clad in a military-style camouflage vest over their long, black garments, and holding semi-automatic rifles in their hands, began to disembark and shoot their way into the hospital, as far as Wunna's eye could see.

'Thanda!' was his first thought.

He ran toward the door of the delivery room, the room he saw Thanda being wheeled in. Banging on it, he shouted, "We're under attack! My wife is there! Please…" his voice trailed off. "Please! Open up!"

He banged the door loudly as the sound of the gunfire began to increase. A nurse ran out, almost slamming into him as she opened the rusting metal door of the delivery rooms.

"Sir, you have to sit down, your wife is not done delivering the baby yet," she turned as she heard Thanda's scream piercing the quiet of the room. "You have to wait here. I will let you know once – "

"We don't have time for this! There are people with guns coming. Can't you hear them shooting?" came Wunna's exasperated reply.

The nurse closed the door behind her. She listened closely, although the sound seemed to be coming from the west side, it was rather faint. But there was no mistaking, it was the sound of gunfire.

Panic arose.

"They don't seem to be far away," she said, shaking in fear, "but we do need to board up the doors of this ward," she added.

Wunna ran to the end of the west hallway. He saw a small utility closet on his way and so he ran in to find something to barricade the door. He fixed his eyes on a large utility cart. The cart had an extension to hold mops and brooms. He took a broom and shoved its handle between the spaces of the door handle in an attempt to hold the doors still.

Meanwhile, the nurse had run to the hallway on the east side. She pulled the fire alarm on her way to try to barricade the stairwell door that was at the end of that hallway. Her plan was simple, to try and alert all the patients, doctors, nurses working in that ward and escort them through the emergency service stairwell. She hoped that the sound itself would alarm the terrorists that were trying to enter the hospital wing they were in.

There were only 10 wards in that unit they were trying to protect. Wunna ran to the other ward doors and tried to evacuate all the patients that were there. Most of them were nursing mothers. As he had managed to evacuate three of the nursing mothers, he saw from the corner of his eye that the nurse that was helping him was struggling to barricade the door, so he ran to her.

"Go and help the others, if you find my wife, please bring her to safety," he demanded.

The nurse nodded and ran to escort the rest of the mothers and their babies through the emergency service stairwell.

The door on the east wing that Wunna was trying to barricade finally gave way.

As if the world had stopped moving, an armed man in a black tunic pointed the gun at Wunna. Wunna was on the ground, propping himself and moving to pick himself up to try to stop his assailant. The whole scenario seemed eerily familiar to him. It was the very incident he tried to stop all those years ago, which had come back to haunt him. Wunna was terrified, but he didn't want to run – not when he felt that his life had only just begun.

He knew that this man in the black tunic was a scout as usually the ones who were willing to put themselves on the front line were the ones that were recently converted into this radical thinking of violence. He felt it in his heart that this man could be talked down to.

'Before the rest come, I must do this,' Wunna vowed.

"STOP!" he shouted. "Please, you don't have to do this!"

"Tell me one good reason why?" the man replied, with a slight coyness in his voice, as he pointed the gun to Wunna's head.

Wunna took a deep breath. He was pinned down and this was his only chance to try and save his family – and himself.

"I know you. I've been here once before, so trust me when I say that this will not end well. More and more people will die. Violence will only beget violence, brother."

"Brother?" replied the man. "Why would you consider me to be one of your own? Especially when I am going to kill you?" he mused.

"We are all the same, and I know that if you find it in your heart – I know that you know what is right. And this? This is never going to end. If you don't stop now, you will lose yourself, and that – that is worse than dying."

The man seemed to consider what he was saying.

"Please, you know you can stop. You don't have to do this," Wunna pleaded.

The man then looked away and for some reason, he began to tear up. He removed the gun and tried to help Wunna up. The sound of single gunfire began to get louder. But alas, a gunshot rang from behind Wunna. He felt a sharp pain searing through his back. He crumpled on the floor and let out a loud cry.

The door that Wunna had initially barricaded on the west side had also finally given way. In the back of his mind he began to think that maybe Thanda hadn't made it as well. All he felt was that he had failed his family. And here, he was going to die. He steadied his breathing, closed his eyes and waited.

The man immediately dipped to check on Wunna.

'*Please be alive*' he hoped. He placed a hand over his wrist, checking for any sign of life.

Wunna slowly opened his eyes.

"Please find my wife," Wunna softly uttered as he reached out to the breast pocket of his tee shirt and passed a photograph to the man in black. He also pulled out the coin that hung around his neck. "You saved me, brother. Take this…" he breathed. The pain was searing and he knew that it was probably his time, "…and remember me," he entrusted the coin to the man in black.

"What the *hell* are you doing Waheed? *Letting this infidel live?*" Wunna's killer asked the man in the black tunic–Waheed. Waheed quickly put the items that Wunna had entrusted him into a vest pocket.

The man shot Wunna one more time, straight to the heart. Waheed turned around, stunned.

"I don't owe you an explanation, Rya," Waheed said as he turned to Wunna's killer and shot him in the head.

At this point, no other terrorists had come through to the hospital unit they were in. At a distance, Waheed could see that there were some nurses who were wounded by gunfire, but they were still escorting some patients that were running for safety. The incessant shrill of the fire alarm was the only thing that felt normal.

Waheed ran towards the other rooms to find the woman in the picture.

***

Thanda had just delivered the baby. She was weak, but she felt relieved that her ordeal was over. The doctor delivering the baby cut the umbilical cord and cleaned him up, placing the baby in a warm bundle on her chest. She was so happy as she saw her son. The baby boy was gurgling and had his eyes open for a moment before he shut them and fell into a peaceful slumber.

At that very moment, Thanda knew that her life was complete. In retrospect, she knew that this was the last moment she had, the last moment of peace, happiness and innocence – before her life changed.

The sound of the fire alarm rang across the room she was in. A doctor ran out to check what the commotion was about. She came back in, looking flushed and afraid. The doctor whispered to the midwife that was in the room. Pointing to Thanda, she whispered to the midwife, "*she and her baby need to get to safety, please bring her out through the emergency exit.*" The midwife nodded.

What was supposed to be a joyful day, had taken an ugly turn. Thanda sensed that there could have been some kind of danger. Her first thought was Wunna. She was hoping that he would be outside, ready to take them and leave whatever danger they were in. She held on to her son tightly as a midwife came to assure that everything was going to be okay.

The midwife took her to the wheelchair at the corner of the room. Thanda clutched her son tightly as she sat on the wheelchair, ready to be wheeled out to safety.

"We are going to see your papa, sweetheart," she whispered to her sleeping son.

As the midwife wheeled Thanda and the baby out, they saw people running across them, towards the emergency stairwell at the end of the hall on Thanda's left-hand side.

"Where is my husband?" Thanda asked the midwife.

"He should be downstairs, almost everyone here is clearing out," came the reply.

As the midwife tried to wheel Thanda to safety, something caught Thanda's line of vision. From the corner of her eye she saw two men in black, with guns. There was a man lying on the floor. She teared up, fearing the worst – that the man on the floor could be Wunna. She then saw one armed man shoot the other. She tried to move away from the midwife who was wheeling her.

"You have to follow me, Miss, please don't be afraid,"

said the midwife as she tried to overpower Thanda's

attempts at resistance.

Somehow, Thanda overpowered the nurse. It was odd

how suddenly she was blessed with the strength to pull

away. She clutched on to her son tightly as she stood

up and walked slowly, crouching in pain – towards a

man in a black tunic with an assault rifle, shooting

another man dressed similarly to him.

Waheed saw this disheveled woman hobbling toward

him. She looked rather young and she had a baby

cradled in her arms. Waheed looked at the photograph

Wunna gave him. If her hair wasn't so messy or her

clothes were not stained with blood, there was no

mistaking it - it was the exact same woman.

Thanda looked at him, in awe and trepidation. He had

a gun. "You shot him…?" she asked weakly.

"He killed a good man," Waheed replied coldly. "The

man he killed – before he died, he told me to find you."

He pointed to the photograph.

It was at this point that Thanda came to a grim

realization that it was all over. Wunna was gone and

nothing would ever be the same again. She always

resented the fact that he had a hero complex; that he

always wanted to do what was right, no matter the cost.

She became angry at the thought that he would put his

life on the line without even thinking about her and

their child.

'Why was he so selfless to the point that he was so

selfish? What about our son?' she questioned.

"You have to come with me," Waheed urged. "I need to get you to safety."

Still tearing, she replied, "How can I trust you?" "How do I know that you didn't kill my husband?" she wailed.

To build some kind of fragile trust, he decided to reveal his identity to her. Waheed took off the black mask that covered his nose and mouth. It revealed a gash across his face, a deep scar that ran from his left cheek to his chin.

"Look, I don't expect you to trust me," he replied. "But if you…" he trailed off, afraid that someone was coming to kill them.

Waheed looked over Thanda's shoulder to see if there was anyone else that he knew was coming to kill her. He gulped in fear of what was to come, if they should ever turn up and find him. He steadied himself, taking a deep breath, he continued, "if you and your baby want to live," he stopped short, as he could hear the sound of gunfire approaching the door behind him. His blood ran cold.

'They're coming. Surely, they will kill us!' he trembled at the thought.

Hearing the faint sound of footsteps that were approaching from behind him, he quickly grabbed a very dazed, angry and confused Thanda by the shoulder and shoved her into the empty storage closet that was unlocked. He then made his way in behind her and closed the door. He left enough space between the door, just enough so that he could see what mayhem was going to unfold.

As Thanda hid in the dark, her thoughts had turned from anger to sadness. She was confused at the events that were unfolding before her eyes. On one hand, she lost the man she loved. On the other hand, another man had come into her life, who claimed he had come to save her. Controlling her physical pain and her emotions, she clutched on to her baby tightly. She was determined to keep him safe, no matter the cost. She was wary about Waheed. But he seemed to be helping her.

All she wanted was for a normal life.

'But that's never going to happen, isn't it?' she wondered.

Waheed pressed his ear against the rickety door of the storage closet. He heard some muffled voices talking.

"Hmmm, they killed Rya too huh?" said one voice.

"Looks like one of ours must have done this," came the muffled reply. This voice was different. It was a lot deeper and it held an emotionless weight to it. "I wonder who had the guts to shoot our best fighter. He must pay for this."

The first voice came back to focus.

"Whoever shot Rya wouldn't have gotten far. Let's just clear this floor and see if we're lucky enough to punish the infidel who shot one of ours," the voice chuckled.

Waheed knew what they meant. They would probably go back to their hideout, in the forest and do a head count — for the men that died for the cause; men like Rya, and men who were M.I.A. Usually the men who went M.I.A were suspected of being unfaithful to the cause. Once they were caught, they were beheaded in front of the camp with a video taken of the execution – that would be displayed for all the world to see, on a world called the internet.

Waheed took a deep breath and peeked through the exposed section of the door. He saw and heard the two men take their leave. They seemed to have been running towards the side of the emergency exit. He slowly opened the door of the closet and poked his head out just to see if they were really gone. He saw their backs turned toward him and they were, true enough, running to the emergency exit. At a distance, he saw one of the men run towards the other wing of the hospital – perhaps to see if there were others they could kill.

Waheed saw that the coast was clear at the door that he first entered from. He motioned to a trembling Thanda to follow him towards their exit in the east wing. He crept through the hallway as Thanda continued to hobble in pain as she followed him. She occasionally looked down to see her baby. He was fast asleep, nestled in the blanket bundle, held by her unsteady arms.

As they passed Wunna and Rya's bodies, the baby had begun to stir softly in his swaddle. Thanda tried to cajole him by rocking him softly. From the corner of her eye, she saw her late husband and his killer. She tried not to weep. She told herself that she had to protect her baby as that is what Wunna would have wanted. She let her tears flow freely as she sobbed silently. They were very close to the exit, almost reaching the door in fact, when the baby scrunched up his little face and began to cry. Thanda and Waheed stopped short.

'*Oh crap!* We're done for,' Waheed panicked.

Thanda tried to comfort her son, but his cries became louder.

"It's over, we are going to die," Waheed gasped.

The two voices that were behind the door, the two men that were scouting the floor they were on ran towards the sound of Thanda's crying baby. Waheed ran in front of Thanda to protect her. He braced himself for an attack, so he turned the safety of his gun off and prepared to defend her. The two men approached.

"So, it was you," said the man with a steely, unfeeling voice. "You killed Rya," he mused.

"It's over for you," said the other man gleefully. "Oh! Such fun we will have biting your head off!"

"And as for you," he eyed Thanda and her baby. "We could find a place for you with us," he smiled coyly.

Waheed looked at them. They were sick, especially the psychopath who wanted to take advantage of Thanda. He could feel his anger coursing through his veins as he stared at them with disgust. He was disgusted at the thought of what would happen to Thanda if they took her. They would enslave her to meet their demands and they would threaten to kill her son if she didn't comply. He was entrusted to protect her, so he tried to put on a brave face. He pointed his gun at the two men.

Little did he know that Thanda was going to be mortified at what she saw. She was afraid at the thought of what these men might do to her. But she also knew that something equally as bad was going to happen. She rocked her little one and braced herself for what was going to happen next.

It all happened too fast – even for Waheed. In one swift motion, as the two other men were discussing their capture, Waheed pulled the trigger and shuddered as two gunshots rang out into each of their heads.

Turning to a shell-shocked Thanda, who was still clutching her crying child, "We have to run, now."

Forgiveness.

'How *on earth* did I get here?' Thanda asked herself as she clutched her son tightly, hobbling behind Waheed.

Adrenaline had got the best of her, masking the pain she was feeling from giving birth. She should have been in bed, resting. But here she was running for her life, with a stranger who should have killed her, but was saving her instead. She felt something warm trickling down her thigh.

'I can't go on, maybe I should just surrender and die here with my baby. It's not like we have a future anyway,' she wept.

Thanda stopped staggering and gave up.

'It's over for us,' she let her sadness take over as she leaned on the wall beside her.

Waheed turned around to see if Thanda was catching up. "Hurry! We are getting close to one of the vehicles!" he exclaimed, motioning Thanda to hurry up.

He saw her weeping, standing at a place where she looked like she was ready to die.

He quickly walked over to her. "Please, miss, I made a vow to keep you and your baby alive. We must escape. You have to hurry."

Thanda continued to grieve but she knew that Waheed was right. She needed to live, not for herself or her child but for Wunna, to keep his memory alive.

'I can't stop grieving, my husband has been taken. But Wunna wanted me and my son to live, and so we shall,' she soldiered on.

Thanda followed Waheed as he took one of the vehicles he had arrived in. The key was still in the ignition.

"Perfect," Waheed muttered as he started the rusty old truck.

From the drivers' seat, he opened the passenger seat door and motioned for Thanda to come in. Clutching her crying baby in one hand, she hastily shut the door. They drove off. The sound of faint gunfire pelted behind them. Waheed looked at the rear mirror only to see that there were some of his ex-comrades who were shooting at them.

'*Crap,*' he swore.

Pressing the accelerator, he drove off hoping to outrun them. The shots were getting significantly louder.

"You have to stay down," he urged Thanda to crouch behind the dashboard.

Waheed checked the rear-view mirror again and saw that they were finally escaping the hospital. The men who were shooting at them were getting smaller. Afraid that someone might follow them, he drove off into a small slip road that led into the forest.

The day was finally coming to an end.

As they were driving in the forest, Thanda and Waheed sat in silence. Thanda was nursing her baby as Waheed drove on the bumpy road that ran through the forest. It was dark and the only sound between them was the occasional bump of the tires and the steady hum of the engine. After what seemed like forever, Thanda finally broke the silence between them.

"Where are we going?" she asked stoically.

"I know a place, a man – my uncle. He lives in this forest," came the tired reply, "he will help you."

They resumed sitting in silence.

The baby started to wean and Thanda quickly buttoned her blouse. She propped up her child, as he was awake. She saw his little face and his little hands, scrunched up into a small, wrinkly ball. He stretched his little arms, closed his eyes and yawned. Thanda re-did his swaddle to keep him warm. She held him close to her chest and gazed at his little face.

'If only you could see your father,' she whispered to her son as he fell back into a peaceful slumber.

Waheed, Thanda, and the baby found themselves at the doorstep of an old but grandiose mansion. Although the exterior of it was fit for a king, it was overgrown with shrubs and vines. The driveway was covered in weeds. The place itself was hidden in the forest, and there were no lights on the porch they were standing on.

Waheed stepped forward, secured his gun and knocked on the ratty door. They could hear someone pounding down a flight of stairs.

"In a minute!" came a muffled voice from inside the house.

The door creaked as it swung open. Waheed took a step back. An elderly man, dressed in a white garment opened the door.

Upon seeing the gun, the elderly man pulled away. "What do you want with me young man?" he quizzed.

"It's me baba, Waheed," he replied.

"Waheed?" he questioned as he looked at Waheed's face with a grim familiarity.

Combing through his memory, he remembered that this young man in front of him was his sister's son. They were very close when Waheed was growing up. Unfortunately, they had lost contact for over a decade. Yet, Waheed's countenance had not faded over the years, if not for the gash across his face.

"How are you?" he finally asked, breaking the silence between them.

"We need your help, baba," he answered, pointing to Thanda and her baby.

"Come in, son," the elderly man motioned, "and you too, young lady."

The elderly man escorted them into the dimly lit house. He led them through a small hallway which led to a living area. There was an old sofa on which he told them to rest on. The elderly man left the room briefly and came back with some candles, dry biscuits and three small water bottles. As Waheed and the elderly man were illuminating the dark room, Thanda held her baby tightly and hoped that the man would help them.

After a few moments, they managed to light the room. The elderly man looked at the two of them and the baby. He motioned to Thanda.

"Can I hold the baby?" he asked.

Thanda was confused but she let the old man hold her son anyway. She gently thrust her baby into the hands of the man as he slowly rocked the sleeping child. Thanda was already weak from the delivery. Losing Wunna, and running out of a warzone were just too much to bear for a day. She was tired and hungry, but she didn't have much of an appetite. The elderly man looked at Thanda and motioned for her to have some of the biscuits.

"Please, you need to eat, you just had a baby!" he exclaimed.

Thanda obliged. The man was right. She had just delivered and she needed to nourish herself so that she could feed the baby.

"Now what can I do for you two?" he asked.

Waheed looked over at Thanda, who was sipping on some water. "She lost her husband today. There was a band of rebels attacking the hospital." He took a deep breath, "I'm not proud to say this. I…I was one of them. I wish I could take everythi…,"

"Why were you one of them?" Thanda hissed as tears streamed down her face.

The elderly man looked forlorn but he was curious to know why his estranged nephew was involved in such a despicable act.

"It's a long story," Waheed winced as he tried to fight

back the tears that were welling up in his eyes.

"Please, son. If you tell us, I can also try to help you,"

the elderly man replied as he cradled the baby.

Waheed fixed his gaze on a burning candle that was on

the table. Maintaining his composure, he started.

"A few years ago, the rebels plundered our village."

***

All Waheed remembered from that day were the loud

sounds of gunfire and makeshift barrel bombs that had

bombarded his village. He saw blood everywhere.

Blood of his parents spilled on the walls and on his

sister, as she rocked back and forth on her heels in a

squatting position – covering her ears and crying, at the

196

corner of the small, one room, zinc roofed hut they lived in. From the corner of his eye, he saw a man clad in black clothes and a green padded vest, holding a long bayonet pointing at his sister's head.

"If you don't comply, we will kill your sister," said the man sharply.

He was terrified. Mira was three years younger to him – fifteen. He didn't want her youth to be taken away from her, 'At least she can have a new life,' he thought. He said that he would follow the man wherever he wanted him to go and do whatever he wanted him to but only on condition that Mira's life would be spared.

The man shoved him and Mira out of the house. Behind them the bombs continued to rage on. One last look over his shoulder before entering the jeep, he saw his house disintegrating in the wave of the bombs. He did not even grief his parents' death – he couldn't

afford to because he knew they would have wanted him

to be strong for Mira.

'I must do this, if not for me, for Mira,' he vowed.

For now, he loved his sister more than life itself.

When they arrived at the camp the man brought them

to, it was dark as night had fallen. All hope was lost for

him. He glanced over at Mira who was still holding his

hand tightly. The camp was relatively small, with about

6 tents built side by side. There was a small bonfire set

in front of one of the yurts on the east side of the

camp. There were men clad in mostly black clothes and

padded vests – like the man who had brought Mira and

Waheed to the campsite, walking about, some with a

cup in one hand, or a cigarette in the other, but all with

a machine gun or a rifle slung over their shoulders. The

man who brought them out of their village motioned to one woman with a veil over her face to take Mira somewhere.

Sensing that they would be separated, Waheed demanded, "Don't you dare take her away from me."

The man retorted. He reached out for his bayonet, that was slung over his right shoulder, and used the sharp end of the knife to silence him. Waheed felt his feet crumble, as he fell to the ground.

"Don't you dare talk to me like that, you hear me?" he growled as he stood over Waheed.

Waheed felt a sharp pain on his left cheek. He could feel heat emanating from that spot. Touching the spot where the searing pain was, he clenched his jaw. He could smell something reminiscent of rusted iron coming out of his skin. The blood had begun to fill his mouth and he leaned forward to cough it out. He could hear Mira crying out. He was beginning to feel lightheaded. As his vision blurred, he saw Mira being taken away by the veiled woman.

He could hear someone saying, "Fix him."

He began to fade out.

***

As he recounted his tale, he surrendered to his grief. There was no point hiding it anymore.

"Once they took us to the camp, they made us do despicable things. It's like we weren't even humans anymore. They made me into a killer. Mira worked the tents where the women were. Like servants to a king, we were there to satisfy them. One day, she just couldn't take it anymore. She tried to escape and they killed her and hung her in front of all the camp to see," Waheed explained, in between sobs.

"When they had planned to attack the hospital, I was thinking of killing the men who killed Mira and running away. Even if they found me and killed me, I would've deserved it anyway. What good life could I give Mira? I thought I could protect her."

"I thought I could protect her," he sobered up. Once again, he sobbed, "I'm sorry, Mira!" he cried in anguish.

Thanda felt sorry for Waheed. Without thinking, she placed her hand softly on his shoulder.

"It's okay," she comforted him.

The old man looked forlorn as he held on to the sleeping child tightly.

"I can't imagine what you went through, son," he shook his head.

Waheed tried to pull himself together.

'Mira would have wanted you to stay strong, stop crying. You have a responsibility to help this woman and her baby – Mira would have wanted that,' he consoled himself.

He wiped the tears from his eyes. Turning to Thanda he said, "I'm sorry I couldn't save your husband."

Thanda stared at Waheed, intently. She shifted her gaze to his fidgeting hands that were shifting between resting on his knees and drying his eyes. She looked back up again at his scar and reached her hand out to touch it. He winced, not because he was offended, but he was taken aback by her reaction.

"I'm so sorry this had to happen to you," she said as she ran her fingers gently along his scar.

***

It had been two days since the escape.

Waheed's uncle had many rooms in his house, of which Thanda and her baby were given one. Thanda was given some of Waheed's uncle's old tunics to change into and some pieces of cloth to make napkins for the baby. Thanda kept busy by feeding the baby, putting him to sleep and grieving the loss of her husband. She spent most of her time in the room she was given.

Waheed's uncle had been coming up to check in on her regularly. He would come in without fail when it was meal time, with a bowl of porridge and some water for her. He would talk to her and after a brief exchange hold the baby and tell her that everything was going to be okay. He would leave only to repeat the same thing the next day. Thanda was glad Waheed's uncle was a nice man.

Waheed kept himself in another room. He still had the photograph and the gold coin that Wunna had entrusted to him. Waheed had all these buried emotions that resurfaced in the past few days. It was causing him to feel hopeless.

'Mira, I've failed you.'

***

Ever since he took his nephew, Thanda, and her child in, Waheed's uncle felt nothing but deep sadness for their stories. He was filled with a sense of responsibility to them. As a cleric of his faith, he realized that what they needed was a miracle – some divine intervention to help them get out of this misery. Waheed's uncle made his way up the ratty, hollow wooden staircase to his study room. The room, although large, held two small bookcases filled with books, religious books and economics and law books, dog-eared and tattered. In front of that book case there was a wooden study table and a rusting metal chair. On the table, there was a landline phone and a small black notebook.

He thumbed through the notebook and found the name '*Emmy Rosenbaum*' written in red. Below the name, there was a phone number to a foreign land. He picked up the phone and dialed the number.

On the second ring, she picked up.

"Emmy?"

"Said? Said, is that you?"

"Yes, it's me, Emmy," Waheed's uncle replied.

"Oh, it's been so long," the voice over the phone
cracked, after a slight pause, "I miss you."

"Emmy, I need a favour,"

"Anything. Just say the word."

And so Waheed's uncle related the story of Waheed,
Thanda and her baby, to Emmy Rosenbaum - his ex-
wife.

He still loved her and so did she. They had a daughter before he went back from England to Pakistan, eventually finding himself in one of his ancestral houses in Thailand.

In the early 70s, Said had made a trip to East Pakistan to visit his ailing father. Unfortunately, they were caught in the border conflict between India and Pakistan, forcing them to flee to their ancestral home in the border town between Thailand and Myanmar. Sadly, Emmy did not hear from her husband for about a couple of weeks and to her horror, was notified that he was dead.

Said was also unable to contact Emmy at the time as his parents and his younger siblings were making their way to Thailand and were trying to get things up and running on their end. And after a series of personal tragedies, it took him a year to reconnect with Emmy.

A tearful Emmy still missed her husband so much and the pressures of taking care of baby Lia - Said and Emmy's daughter, were apparent. Knowing that Said now had to take care of his family after his father's death, he asked her to wait a little longer for him to be reunited with her back in England. For Said, leaving Emmy and his daughter, Lia, was the worst thing that happened in his lifetime.

Emmy promised to wait and Said used to call Emmy up very often. He would talk to her and Lia. However, as time went on, it was apparent to Emmy that Said would never return and after six years of waiting, Emmy felt that it was time for her to move on from Said, even though she still loved him and wanted to be with him.

Emmy had full custodial rights to their daughter. But as much as Emmy tried, she never could move on from Said. And after all those years of talking on the phone, they still loved each other. Still, there was nothing she wouldn't do for him and there was nothing he wouldn't do for her. When Emmy heard the story, she felt overwhelmed. She knew that her husband's heart was in the right place and she was compelled to do something for Thanda and her baby.

"Darling, I'll speak to a friend. He can help with Thanda's case."

"Thank you, Emmy," he replied feebly.

***

Waheed sat alone in his room. Night had fallen and he sat in darkness. His uncle had just spoken to him about

Thanda and the baby, mentioning that there was

someone who would help them. Waheed was relieved

knowing that they were going to be safe after all. He

got up from his rattan bed and flipped the light switch

on. He reached into the drawer of a small bedside table

where he kept the coin and photograph that Wunna

had entrusted to him before he was brutally killed.

Thumbing the coin, Waheed closed his eyes.

'Kind sir, you showed me kindness even though I was

supposed to kill you. Thank you for showing me that

I'm not lost. Your wife and your son – I'm sure if you

could see them now, you would be proud of them.

They are safe. They are brave, just like you,' he thought.

"Here's to you, kind stranger," he whispered.

Waheed got up from his bed. He grabbed the photograph with the coin and knocked on the ratty old door down the hall. Thanda opened it and motioned to him to keep silent. She looked like she had been crying. Her eyes were tired and she had a towel wrapped over her head.

"I just put him down to sleep," she whispered to Waheed as she pointed to her baby.

She removed the damp towel from her head and dried her hair as she sat on the floor next to the bed. Waheed followed suit. Sitting across from her, he leaned against the wall.

"So, what brings you here?" she quizzed.

"I just came to pass you some things that I believe belong to you," he replied, thrusting the photograph and the gold coin necklace to Thanda.

She looked down at the items on her palm. It made her tear up. She took a deep breath and tried to regain her composure.

"Your husband – he gave them to me," he shifted his gaze toward the floor. "He told me to find you and pass this to you."

Thanda let the tears stream down her cheeks.

"Thank you," she mouthed. Drying her eyes, she continued. "He told me that this coin was given to him by a woman who lived in the forest in Myanmar. She was the mother of a man who my husband killed. Although he did it in self-defence, Wunna – my husband, saw it as an act of violence." Thanda lifted the coin up, "he wanted to come clean, but the woman forgave him."

Waheed listened intently.

"I don't blame you for what happened that day – at first I did, but I realized that you were just a victim. Because my husband taught me how to forgive, I'm forgiving you, too," Thanda said.

***

"I'm forgiving you, too," were the words that rang in Waheed's head as he lay awake that night on his bed.

He recounted the conversation he had with Thanda just a few hours ago. He felt free. For as long as he could remember, he was feeling so guilty. From the time his parents had died and during the time of his capture, he had been feeling guilty and ashamed for all the actions that he had taken to preserve his and Mira's life. Saving Thanda gave him some purpose and being forgiven by her felt liberating. Yet, he still felt that he had to pay his dues as a penance for all that he had done to inflict harm upon innocent people.

'But isn't that what forgiveness is all about? An unconditional surrender for all the things you've done in the past?' he deliberated.

He got out of bed and walked down the hall to the study room his uncle was still in. He lingered outside the room, hesitant to ask about what Thanda mentioned about forgiveness. But he needed to know if he was worth being forgiven. As the door was left ajar, from the corner of his eye, the old cleric spotted Waheed at the door.

"Son?" he called out.

Waheed pushed open the rickety wooden door. He still stood by the doorway.

"Baba, I…," he trailed off.

'Where do I begin?' he pondered.

"Son, what is it?" Said asked.

Waheed cleared his throat. "Baba, what does forgiveness mean?"

The cleric removed his reading glasses and looked at Waheed, puzzled. "What do you mean?" came the startled reply.

"Forgiveness…" he trailed off, walking towards his uncle. "Baba, what is forgiveness?"

The cleric looked at his nephew. "Son, forgiveness is when people let go of the hurt they feel. It is when people realise that there's no point holding on to whatever pain they have."

"For the pain I've caused?" Waheed quizzed.

"Yes, and sometimes, the only way to forgiveness, is to forgive yourself."

Hope.

Thanda sat alone in the room. A naked bulb illuminated the room. Her baby was sleeping soundly, bundled up under a warm blanket on a mat. She looked at him as he slept soundly, observing his breathing. She saw everything she wanted and everything she lost. All she wanted was a quiet life, with Wunna and her baby. She just wanted a family.

Thanda was still in pain from her delivery and her blood-soaked *sarong* was in a small pail soaking in bleach. Thinking about that made her cry. That was the last thing Wunna saw her in. He would never have the chance to see her in anything ever again. Her son would not have a father and neither would she have an opportunity to give Wunna a decent burial or even to say goodbye. She succumbed to her emotional pain as her mind dwelt on these things and wept again.

The night had passed, painfully and slowly for Thanda.

***

The next morning, Thanda was hastily awakened by a knock on her room door.

Her eyelids shot open, 'Wunna?' she thought.

The knock got louder.

"It's me, Uncle Said" came the muffled voice.

"Uncle, come in," Thanda got up from her mat and she opened the ratty wooden door as she rubbed her eyes to wipe the sleep from her eyes.

The old cleric stood by the door. "Thanda, there is something I want to tell you," he said.

Thanda looked at him, "yes, uncle?" she asked.

"Thanda, I've been talking to a friend of mine," he said. "She, uh, well, she's my wife, ex-wife," he continued, rocking back and forth on his heels.

"Uncle, what is this about?" Thanda asked gently.

"Thanda, I have found a way I can help you and your baby," the cleric said quietly. "Emmy, my wife, has a friend who says you can find a safe place in another part of the world."

"Where?" Thanda asked.

"I'm not too sure of the details," the cleric replied, "but Waheed has agreed to drop you off at the airport in the Capital tomorrow. As far as I know there will be someone there who will help you and the baby find a safe passage."

Thanda couldn't believe what she was hearing. When the cleric left, she closed the door of her room and sat on the mat where her sleeping baby was laid on. She gently reached out to carry him. He shifted restlessly around in her arms and opened his eyes. She looked at her son and stroked his soft, ruddy cheeks with the back of her index finger. He blinked and he started to cry.

"Aww baby, yes, I know darling," she comforted him, unbuttoning the top of the shirt she was wearing and placed the child in a comfortable position to nurse him. She cradled him tenderly as he fed.

She kept thinking about what the cleric had said about her and her baby leaving for another land. A part of her was sad and the other part was hopeful for a better future. She couldn't stop thinking about Wunna, still desperately wishing that he was with her at this point.

'If he was here I wouldn't even need to be in this situation,' she contemplated. 'Oh, God, what should I do?'

***

Meanwhile, Waheed was on the floor of his uncle's study thinking about Thanda.

'She must leave tomorrow, for her and her child's safety,' his uncle's words repeated in his mind all morning since he told Waheed the news.

Waheed felt a sense of duty to care and protect Thanda and her son. He wanted her to know that he was thankful that she extended forgiveness to him; that she understood him despite all the atrocious things he had done.

He sat there pondering on his uncle's words of forgiveness and what it meant to forgive himself. He closed his eyes and prayed.

"God, I am a sinner, I don't know whether I deserve your love but I see your forgiveness through Thanda. I thank you for that," he prayed aloud. "But I don't know if I can ever forgive myself."

***

"I don't know if I can ever forgive myself."

Thanda heard these words uttered as she walked past Waheed's uncle's study. Curious, she peeked in through the gap of the half-closed door.

"Waheed?" she called out.

His eyes snapped open. "Thanda!" he gasped.

"I'm sorry, I didn't mean to startle you," she apologised. Looking at his clasped hands, and his posture facing Mecca, "I didn't know you were praying."

"No, no, it's fine!" he said quickly, he got up from his prayer mat and sat on the floor near the window.

Leaning at the doorway, Thanda watched him and asked, "Why do you feel that you're not deserving of forgiveness?"

"I don't know," Waheed replied feebly. "I just… I mean I've done a lot of things that hurt others. I feel like…" He took a deep breath and collected his thoughts. "I don't deserve to be here, or to live when I've hurt so many people who didn't deserve to die," he shuddered as tears welled up in his eyes.

Thanda walked closer to him and put her arm around him in a warm embrace. "When you forgive yourself, it's not like you will magically forget all the things you have done. You'll still remember them and it will hurt, but in time you will feel free."

"Why?"

"I don't know," Thanda replied. "But all I know is that when you learn to let it go, all the unforgiveness, hatred and pain, when you look back one day, the memory won't hurt as much."

Thanda pulled away, getting up to leave.

"Don't let go," Waheed beckoned, with tears streaming down his face. "Please?"

She sat down and embraced him one more time.

***

That night, Thanda lay awake on her mat next to her baby. After contemplating the series of events and forgiving Waheed, she felt a sense of peace. It was strange how she felt a sense of hope with all the sadness and pain around her. Feeling exhausted, she closed her eyes and took a deep breath and fell into a fitful slumber.

"Thanda, Thanda, it's me, where are you?"

She heard a voice that sounded like Wunna's.

"Wunna is that you?" she called out.

"Thanda, wake up, you have to make a decision!" the voice echoed.

Thanda opened her eyes and all she saw were stalks of tall grass. She propped herself up on her elbows and looked towards the horizon of an empty field - beyond the grass that was blocking her view. It was bright as the sun was rising. She was alone.

"Wunna, where are you?" she asked as she turned around.

"There you are!" Wunna exclaimed. "I've been looking all over for you!"

"All over for me? All there is, is grass. I thought it would be easy to find me," she retorted.

"I see some things never change," Wunna smirked. "I've missed you, your quick wit, your humour. Where have you gone?" he asked as he sat next to her.

She leaned in and rested her head on his shoulder. "I missed you too," she replied, biting her lower lip to prevent herself from bawling her eyes out.

She looked at Wunna, studied the side of his face, "I wish you were here with me to make this decision, I cannot do this alone," she whispered.

"I know it is not going to be easy but, I know that you will make the right decision. You will do what is best for our son."

Wunna turned to face her as he stood up. "I have to go now Thanda,"

"Please don't leave me," she said as tears rolled down her sunken cheeks. "Don't leave...please?" she pleaded, grabbing onto his arm.

Wunna reached out and helped her up to her feet. He pulled her into his warm embrace. He held her as she buried her face in this chest.

He leaned forward and whispered in her ear, "I have to go now, but I will see you again. I will always love you Thanda. Always!"

Wunna and Thanda shared a quick kiss, after which Wunna turned away, and walked in the direction of what appeared to her as a light, brighter than the mid-day sun. Wunna walked towards the light until he faded away from her vision.

"Goodbye, love."

***

"Are you ready to leave?" Waheed's uncle asked Thanda.

"Yes," she replied as she pointed to a small suitcase that he had given her.

"Now, these are some immigration forms that you will have to fill out when you meet Emmy's friend at the Airport," he said as he gave her a clear plastic folder. "I know you don't have your documents, but this should help."

"Thank you for everything, Uncle," she said.

"Hey, don't mention it," he said. "If it were down to you I know you would do the same for me."

Thanda smiled. With the baby in one hand, she hugged Said in the other.

"You have been like a father to me these past few days," she said. Tears were running down her cheeks but she was happy. She was at peace. "Thank you, truly."

They pulled away.

"Are you ready?" Waheed asked again as he walked towards the main door. "The truck is ready, just let me know when you are," he said as he opened the main door and walked out towards the pick-up truck.

He took her suitcase and placed it in the backseat.

"I should probably go," said Thanda as she looked over her shoulder at the open main door of the house.

"Yes dear, a new life awaits you," said Waheed's uncle.

Thanda clutched her baby in one hand and the folder containing the immigration forms in the other, as she walked out of the door, full of hope for a better future.

A new life awaited her indeed.

Epilogue.

The cream-colored hospital room rasped silently. The machine breathed a steady hum, a slow beat that lasted not more than 3 seconds. A crude beep rang almost every two seconds, breaking the silence when it could – cruelly reminding Thanda of her mortality. There were soft voices – whispering words of comfort to one another. A small crowd had gathered around a hospital bed.

Next to the bed, there was a small bedside table that enshrined Thanda's life. A palm-sized frame held an old, faded wedding photograph of her and Wunna. Smaller pictures of Thanda's friends, grandchildren, a few of her trinkets, necklaces and rings were strewn over the table. There was the Bible, which Wunna referred to as the leather book. He would flip it from time to time and listen intently to the bible stories that Thanda would tell him. Distant memories came to life by that bed side, that kept her company for the past

month she had been in the hospital.

It had been fifty-eight years since she lost Wunna and

not a day went by where Thanda didn't think of him.

Age had caught up with her, but her memory had been

as clear as the day she first met him. She savoured

every bit of her life but she was waiting for this

moment – she was ready.

The years had been kind to her, although there was

sadness, pain and loss. She had been blessed with her

one and only child, whom she called Ming - after her

brother, who loved her with all his life, but left her

behind to be with Wunna. Cancer had taken him in his

fortieth year on earth. He left behind three children and

a wife for Thanda to take care of. Thanda herself had 6

great-grandchildren of her own, a couple of in-laws - all

of them supportive and loving.

She had lived a full life.

"Come here," Thanda rasped, signalling for a young man in the crowd of her friends and family – the youngest of all the great-grandchildren.

He moved towards her, slightly forlorn. His eyes were holding back tears. He took a deep breath and ran his fingers along his short, dark hair. He closed his eyes and let a tear fall down his cheek. He was desperately trying his best to fight back his tears. The woman he loved was leaving. He walked over to the bed and knelt beside her.

"Colin, my dear," she took a deep breath, "this is for you" she motioned to the necklace on the bedside table.

"Mama? This one?" he asked as he picked up a

necklace – a plain black cloth chain that held a gold,

coin-like, pendant.

"Mhm, yes," she nodded. "Take it. It's for you.

Remember me, and remember, this coin is not all about

me. My Wunna taught me how to love, to forgive and

to care for one another – just as I cared for you." She

took a deep breath. "This coin is a reminder of all that,

and I want you to have it Colin."

Colin sobbed. He heaved heavily as the tears fell from

his eyes. He looked up at Thanda, on bended knee –

with the coin in one hand and another holding her frail,

wrinkled, but strong hands. She looked at him and

cupped his chin with her free hand. He looked up, with

his soft grey eyes – reminiscent of her late husband.

She wiped away his tears.

"I have to go now," she whispered.

Colin gently held her hand. "No, mama. Please…" he choked. "I need you."

Thanda looked over at Colin, and then at the crowd that came to say goodbye. From the corner of her eye she saw a bright light illuminating the room, almost blinding her vision. Out of that bright light she saw a young man step out. He was clothed in a soft shirt and a grey pair of pants – the last thing he wore when she last saw him. Her eyes were filled with hope and wonder because she remembered him.

"Wunna…" she trailed off. A single tear rolled down her cheek. She smiled and closed her eyes, embracing the light that ran across the room.

The machine stopped beeping. The room fell into a

moment of silence.

Gold Coin

Acknowledgements.

I would like to thank my parents, Lydia and Ravi for all their support in this journey called life. It was never an easy one for me, but they did everything they could to love and care for me. I will always remember them as a true inspiration for what unconditional love means in my life. I would also like to thank my sister, Ishvareya - without her I would literally be at a loss. I am thankful to God for blessing me with her in my life. She may not have been born of the same blood, but I can confidently say that she is my sister for life. Her support throughout this project means the world to me. I would also like to dedicate this book to my closest confidants, Hannah, Si Hui, Tika, Izza, Matt, Jasmine, Sharon, Cheryl, Choi and Kenn who stood by me throughout my most challenging times and encouraging me. Thank you lovely folks for listening to my rants and the copious amounts of coffee and conversations that we have had – I am truly blessed.

I would also like to dedicate this book to the beautiful people of Myanmar. I know the road hasn't been easy for them, considering all that has happened. But I am sure, as long as the sun rises, so will your strength in demanding justice, peace and a better future. I will always be blessed and encouraged by your strength.

Last but not the least, I am truly grateful to God for sending His Son, Jesus into the world so that I can experience eternal life through His death on the Cross. This is the life that Thanda walked into as she departed and someday, I know, those who trust Jesus will also do the same. Although I feel a sense of sadness being here, living in these strange and uncertain times. I am also glad that this soul got to see life in all its pain and in all its glory.